STRANGE
BEDFELLOWS

STRANGE BEDFELLOWS

Pat Boran was born in Portlaoise in 1963. His stories and poems have appeared in many magazines and have been broadcast on BBC and RTE radios, where he has been among the finalists in the Francis MacManus Awards for short stories. In 1988 he was chosen as a BBC Young Playwright for his play, *Not Dead But Lifeless*. His first collection of poetry, *The Unwound Clock*, won the Patrick Kavanagh Award in 1989. He is at present living in Dublin.

By the same author

Poetry

The Unwound Clock (Dedalus Press, 1990)

History and Promise (International University Press, 1990)

STRANGE BEDFELLOWS

PAT BORAN

·SALMON·

PUBLISHING

First published in 1991 by
Salmon Publishing, Bridge Mills, Galway.

ISBN   0 948339 65 9   Softcover   £6.50
ISBN   0 948339 64 0   Hardcover   £9.50

Acknowledgements are due to the editors
and producers of the following where a number
of these stories originally appeared:

*New Irish Writing (The Sunday Tribune);
Edible Houses (Dublin); Image; Passages (Belfast);
RTE Radio 1; Morning Story (BBC Radio 4).*

The author wishes to thank Mary and Bernard Loughlin
of the Tyrone Guthrie Centre at Annaghmakerrig, and
George Steinmann and Henry Levy of Kulturzentrum
BINZ 39, Switzerland, where a number of these stories
were written.

Cover by Michael Boran.
Typeset in New Century Schoolbook.
Printed by Colour Books, Dublin.
Hardback binding by Kenny's Book Binding, Galway.

CONTENTS

FREDDIE'S BABY

And they all lived happily ever after.

Freddie looked up to see the tiny hand close and reopen over the invisible objects he imagined even now flitted across its palm. He closed Renagh's story book and put it down lightly on the floor. As always he had the feeling that her sleeping world, for all its phantoms, might somehow yet be more real, more coherent, than the one which he inhabited. He considered this a while. But, remembering the night's work which lay ahead of him, he dimmed the light to a warm glow and left the room.

'Are you nearly ready?'

'Nearly,' Freddie called down. There were 30 or so pages of the manuscript still to go and he was further slowed by the printer's manual feed. The morning light bleached his study, made it look like some impersonal hospital waiting room. Freddie, standing before the mirror, might have been the patient, so tired and sickly did he appear after his sleepless night.

He rubbed a hand over his bristled face. He knew he should have shaved during the night's wait. Now, there wasn't time. Tired, and with his ulcer acting up again, he would have to attend the meeting looking like a hobo or Yasser Arafat. This, of course, was the computer's fault. Freddie needed perfect copy today and had no choice but to humour the infernal machine. Professional publishers, he knew, were irritated by those dot matrix printouts—sometimes running into their hundreds and hundreds of pages. He did not believe that busy publishing executives bothered to persist with semi-legible manuscripts. And why should they? Freddie empathized. He had the same problem himself. It was the least he could do, to go to the trouble of presenting his work with care. If *he* didn't care for it, who *would?* If that was all he had learned, he had learned something from those expensive correspondence courses which Brenda had enrolled him in the previous year as a birthday present.... (Thirty-nine and still at school, Renagh had teased. Little swine, retorted Freddie.)

This morning, however, low though he might have been feeling, the fruits of his labours were at least evident. The final pages of his latest novel rolled off, well if not the presses, then at least off the word processor. Any writer would have been proud of such a beautifully produced manuscript. And rightly so. No one could fault those margins, those paragraphs, that hyphenation. The pagination was breathtaking! Not once did he break a sentence over successive pages. Every page had his name on the top, *and* the name of the story. His covering letter was brief (though he had included a 7-page curriculum vitae at the back, just in case), and there was a stamped self-addressed envelope enclosed.

The printer screeched its way back and forth over the lines.

'Very nearly...' He stood at the top of the stairs and watched his nine-year-old daughter emerge from her room to pass him on her way to the bathroom. Her hair was standing up comically on one side of her head.

'Sleep well?' Freddie asked. 'All ready for the journey?' He was full of hope, if exhausted.

Renagh said nothing.

'Did Freddie's computer disturb you?' He tried to sound intimate through the bathroom door. 'Freddie's sorry, Ree, but the publishers like their margins.'

Inside, the toilet flushed and he heard the catch on the door draw back.

'Some publishers like their margins hard, Ree, others like them soft.' Freddie took to whispering at the keyhole when she did not appear. 'I like them rare to well done myself.'

'Knock knock.'

'Who's there?'

'Renagh.'

'Renagh who?' Freddie could already see her grin in his mind's eye.

The door opened.

'Renagh pretty ballerina.' She poked him in the stomach but slipped away when he tried to catch her.

'Will that printing take all day? We have a train to catch.' She slammed the bedroom door.

'How they grow up, Brenda,' said Freddie downstairs. 'She's a woman already.'

'Are you finished yet?' Brenda spoke without looking away from the soap opera on the portable television. She could think of better ways of spending her day off work than sitting round the kitchen.

'Yes, are you nearly ready?' said Renagh, coming into the kitchen, suddenly dressed.

Freddie stepped backwards, clutching at the towel rack. 'I am dying with love for both of you.' He croaked something more and slid down the wall to the floor. Renagh watched patiently to see if there would be a stain of ketchup left behind. There wasn't.

'Almost there, ladies,' Freddie said, jumping up, knowing he had lost his audience. With a bound he was on his way upstairs to feed the waiting machine.

'Where are we?'

'Fade Street.' Freddie's voice fell to a whisper.

'Where's that?'

'I don't know. Why don't we go down here and ask someone.'

'Why don't we—' began Renagh, but she thought it better to stop short.

'Now, we'll have none of that, my love,' said Freddie, sensing her mood. 'We'll be in and out of here before you know it, and then we'll go off somewhere nice to eat before meeting up with your mother again.'

'Mummy would have known the way. She wouldn't be lost,' said Renagh.

'Hush. Someone down here will tell us.'

'She wouldn't be lost. She *knows* things.'

Freddie stopped in his tracks.

'Listen here, young lady, I know quite a few things too, as well as your mother.'

'What do you know, Freddie?'

Freddie thought. Even though he knew her form well by now he was always stumped when she stood up to him like that. People whose eyes were on a level with his

4

belly button should not, he knew, present him with organizational difficulties.

'Well, I know... what your dreams were about last night,' he said with an air of satisfaction.

'What?'

'Beanstalks! I saw your hands clutching after them again.'

Renagh pulled her fists together the very way her mother did when she was gearing herself up for some declaration.

'I did not. I dreamed about how to build huge bombs and guns and scare meanies into giving money to their kids. I want some money now and I want to go around on my own and not talk stupid talk to people in offices....'

'Ree!' Freddie scolded. 'Where ever did you get a notion like that? Don't let your mother hear that kind of talk. It isn't nice. Not nice at all. What you dreamed about was beanstalks from the story.'

'No such thing!' Renagh huffed, and stamped her feet.

Freddie could see he was getting nowhere, so he hooked her by the arm and drew her reluctantly down the street. He would be late for his appointment. What had become of childlike innocence, he wondered?

'Is,' he said after a time, '*is* such a thing.' He had had enough of the silence. But Renagh resisted the bait.

They pressed through a crowd and emerged in a street which Freddie recognized with some relief. They were only a block or two off course. Renagh's mood seemed to improve a little, but Freddie couldn't help but wonder what it was about him that her quick eyes were recording for future use.

It was raining when they reached the building. Renagh had hardly spoken since their earlier exchange. Freddie, now out of breath, his heart beating madly, examined the brass plate for a moment or two and then pressed the bell. Brass plates had a funny effect on him. They brought on fits of cold sweat. Always he had to remind himself: this is not a surgery or an accountancy firm or a court. He pressed a button, gave his name and the voice on the intercom invited him up. He warned Renagh to be on her best behaviour. There was little playfulness now in his voice.

'I'm here to see Mr Wordsworth,' said Freddie to the receptionist. He held the manuscript discretely, but still in such a way that she could not miss seeing it. He was an author. He came bearing his manuscript. He had nothing to be ashamed of.

The receptionist began to make some excuse. 'Mr Wordsworth, I'm afraid, is...'

At the glass-topped coffee table behind him, Renagh was leafing furiously through the old Sunday supplements. The receptionist fell silent. She looked beyond Freddie in horror.

Freddie turned to find Renagh holding aloft a nude double-spread of Marilyn Monroe.

'What do you think, Freddie?' she screwed up her face, tilting her head this way and that. 'What do *you* think, miss?'

Freddie reddened. 'Perhaps if he could spare a minute or two, just two or three minutes....'

The receptionist did her best to join him in ignoring the girl. The parents in these situations, she probably told herself, usually know best what to do. But the tearing sounds coming from Renagh's direction broke her concentration more than once.

'I'm afraid you really should have made an appointment, Mr—'

'Horseman. Freddie Horseman. Surely you remember the...'

'Mr Horseman. He's very busy.' She produced something from under her desk. 'However, he has left me this... to return to you should you call around... and offers his apologies.' She handed Freddie a manuscript, almost identical to the one he had brought with him and had just placed before him. There was an embarrassed silence.

He looked at the brown paper bag in his hand. He looked at the tastefully decorated reception area, the neat desks, the tidy clothes of the receptionist. He was careful not to look around at Renagh.

'He's finished with it already?'

'I'm sure he explains everything in the letter,' said the receptionist.

'Yes,' Freddie said. 'I'm sure that's it. He must have felt it would be more suitable for another publishing house. Mr Wordsworth is always very generous to me with his advice. He's particular, your boss is very particular, not to publish books which should appear from a specialist publisher. He knows the importance of specializing. Few publishers do, you know.'

He considered some more. 'I won't read this now. I'll wait until I get home, until I have time to study the suggestions in detail.' He was unable to conceal his disappointment.

'You *will* give him the new one meanwhile?'

'Yes,' said the receptionist.

'The brown bag!' Renagh, who was stuffing the Monroe picture into her pocket, interrupted. 'Lose it, Freddie. It looks like something they send dirty books in.'

Freddie tensed: she had gone too far this time.

'A suggestion,' said Renagh, 'that's all.'

Freddie avoided the receptionist's eye but studied the package she was holding. He considered it for a moment, retrieved it and weighed it in his hand. 'Right...' He removed the brown paper bag, checked the elastics that were holding the 388 pages together and left the manuscript down on the desk with an unnecessary thump.

'Happy?' he turned to Renagh. 'Neat enough for you?'

'Ninety-three thousand, five hundred and eighteen words,' Renagh beamed at the receptionist. 'I'll say it's neat.'

In that moment Freddie forgave her everything.

'Seven characters, fifteen locations, a science fictionology enigma for thriller lovers,' he continued. And then, turning to the receptionist: 'This is the one that will do it. This time. Mark my words.'

The receptionist smiled wanly.

'Want to hear the title? Are you ready for this?' Freddie struck the manuscript again with his open hand, for effect.

'*Do Theoretical Physicists Exist?* The shout caused the receptionist to take a couple of steps back from her desk for safety.

'Exist!' echoed Renagh in her loudest voice. She dashed over and stood beside Freddie on her toes. Sometimes she liked his craziness, but there was so little of it.

'What do you think of that? *Do Theoretical Physicists Exist?*' In his enthusiasm Freddie had forgotten his earlier fall-out with his daughter and lifted her now onto the reception desk so that the three of them could share the joke.

'Mr Horseman,' a voice said coolly, 'Wordsworth & Sons do not publish science-fiction. Teach yourself books—accountancy, gardening, flower arranging—not science fiction.'

'Science fact-fiction, fiction-fact,' Freddie persisted, turning to the newcomer. 'Categories! All I need is someone, the right publishing house, don't misunderstand me, to have a close look at it, at the whole *opus*. If I get that I'll catch a fish, I'll catch one, I'll catch ten, a hundred. This is a brave, a revolutionary book.'

'I'm sure it is. And how are you these days?' The man extended a soft hand which had never experienced hardship.

'Well, don't take my word,' said Freddie, looking at the hand as if he couldn't quite remember what it was for. 'Read it for yourself. It's got block-buster written all over it.'

'More like block-head,' Renagh sniggered to the receptionist. The receptionist, somewhat taken aback by the girl's sudden change of allegiance, left her station and removed to the coffee table to rearrange the magazines.

'We're very sorry,' said Mr Wordsworth as he walked Freddie and Renagh to the street. 'Really, Mr Horseman—Freddie—you'll have to separate some of these strands. You can't just bung it *all* in there. *You* might know what they're about, but you're the only one who does. There must be at least five different stories mixed up in that last one.'

'I know,' said Freddie, misunderstanding. 'It's wonderful, isn't it?'

Mr Wordsworth kept his patience. 'Think about it,' he said. 'Do that much for me.'

Freddie nodded, pretending to consider the advice. He pretended for what he thought was a realistic amount of time. Then he continued.

'Will you ring me and let me know? There might be someone else interested in having a look at it.' He was aware as he said it that the lie was unmistakeable for what it was.

'I will,' said Mr Wordsworth, letting him off the hook. 'I'll ring if I like it.'

'I've even got some ideas for the cover.'

'I'll ring,' said Mr Wordsworth, patiently.

'It made *me* stay up all night,' Freddie shouted back down the street as he was dragged off by Renagh. 'It's unputdownable!'

Mr Wordsworth stood expressionlessly in the doorway, letting the midday traffic flow into a blur before him. 'Rubbish,' he muttered as he headed back towards his quiet office.

The record skipped each time Renagh jabbed the buttons on the jukebox.

'Hey!'

Freddie looked up from the letter at the barman.

'That kid should be on a lead.'

'That barman should be in a kennel,' retorted Renagh.

'Renagh!' Freddie abandoned his triple bacon, lettuce and tomato sandwich and went over to lead her out of temptation.

'Don't mess!'

The barman addressed the other customers. 'Imagine raising a kid like that?'

'She's not mine,' apologized Freddie. He had not meant to say it. 'Well, not originally,' he added, awkwardly.

The barman moved off.

'This man is not my daddy,' said Renagh.

Freddie looked around hurriedly. 'Can you keep it down? Ree, there are people here who don't know us, you know. You know?' The acidity in his stomach made him belch.

'Look,' he said, holding aloft the glass, 'would you like another?'

'Makes me piss,' said Renagh, defiantly.

Freddie gave her another 20p for the jukebox and returned to his food. There was still the rest of the afternoon to go before they would meet up with Brenda. It seemed likely that he would need all his strength.

After the amusement arcades, the three acid house boutiques full of tie-dye shirts in purples and reds, and a couple of stop-offs at newsagent shops along the way to see if the week's pop papers were in yet, Freddie and Renagh arrived at the designated store where they would meet up with Brenda. Freddie was foot-sore and irritable. He had dropped his manuscript in a scramble across a zebra crossing, and the unnumbered pages had spilled from the unsealed envelope. 'Because of the extreme modernism of this particular work,' he again tried to explain the gravity of the situation to Renagh, 'it may never be possible to replace the fragments in the original sequence.' Renagh said nothing. Freddie remained red in the face for some minutes, and then he too fell silent.

From time to time as they stood in front of the shop window they attracted the curious looks of passers-by and others waiting at the famous city centre meeting place. The clock over Renagh's head chimed five, signalling that Brenda was half an hour late. Renagh looked at Freddie; Freddie returned the look. To one side an elderly lady studied them. Renagh began shifting restlessly. Freddie frowned. The woman looked at Renagh, then at the middle-aged man with the brown envelope under his arm. Renagh looked at Freddie, then at the woman. The woman smiled and approached.

'Are you all right, love?' she began.

'This man...' said Renagh.

Freddie pursed his lips.

'This man is not my daddy.'

The elderly woman looked quizzically at Freddie. Freddie smiled weakly, about to speak.

'He's holding me against my will.'

'Now, Ree,' Freddie cautioned. 'Hello—'

'Back!' The woman tensed. Freddie froze. She held an umbrella at stomach height and he was taking no chances with what was left of his digestion.

'I'll use it.'

'He's not my daddy. He's kidnapped me!' Renagh seized the opportunity. 'He's got dirty pictures in that envelope!'

She dived at the envelope and knocked it from Freddie's grasp. For the second time that afternoon *Do*

12

Theoretical Physicists Exist? spilled out randomly in the street. Renagh looked down at the mess and laughed in horror at what she had done.

As Brenda came down the escalator inside the store with her arms full of a new coat, and a tweed hat for Freddie, outside she could see a crowd of people had gathered.... And Renagh and Freddie.... And a policeman! She ran towards the door.

Freddie stood back after repeated requests from the policeman. The girl would tell her side of the story. To his amusement, he found himself wondering what the chances were that the novel had reassembled itself in the second fall.

AND THE STREET WENT BLIND

Labourers don't spit for the same reasons as the rest of us. Granted theirs is thirsty work, work which demands the regular clearing of the mouth and throat; but their spitting is also a salutation, an ice-breaker, a ritual of friendship. I tried to remind myself of this as they spat upon my arrival by taxi, spat upon my approach across the hazardous stew of mud and stones which comprised the site, spat as one of the younger ones forced his last cigarette on me. We puffed in silence, wondering what to make of each other. An old woman and her dog linked past where we stood in the sun, surrounded by the half-demolished buildings of an area which my memory insisted was home.

'Ten minutes,' said a tall one whom I presumed to be the foreman. He spat uncomfortably. 'It's just that we've got our orders.' And he walked over to where the others had gathered for a tea-break, absently tapping a spoon which he'd produced from his pocket against the side of his leg.

'C'mon,' they were shouting impatiently, while one or two had already sugared and stirred with the handles of screwdrivers or whatever.

The foreman stopped and turned:

'Ten minutes, mind.'

'Spoon, spoon, spoon,' they chorused, banging their tin cups on the oil-drum table.

It had been my father's place—an optician's, if you could call it that—in the beginning anyway. Pieces of broken spectacles lay covered in dust in the big window which was shaped like an eye. At one time the whole city recognized it, commented on its aptness, would discuss the peculiar feeling of finding one's own reflection in the glass, as if the city were constantly watching.

We'd started out a long time before, selling spectacles—ok, we'll call them glasses—which we kept in a shoe box on the counter of our general store. The glass was already in them when you arrived. You simply selected the ones you felt you could see best with from the range. If one of the lenses was damaged (as was often the case), or simply unsuitable, my father would switch it with one from another pair. No problem. Frames with both lenses damaged he gave to an army of old beggars patrolling the inner-city streets, who seemed delighted to stumble about, crashing over dustbins. In the beginning he had simply removed the useless lenses and given them the unwanted empty frames, but they had felt deceived and were, in any case, happier to suffer what they obviously felt was 'strong medicine'.

My job, charging in from school with a mouthful of sherbet, was to keep the precious lenses clean and, if possible, intact after their often severe handling. There was also the important duty of keeping all convex lenses out of direct sunlight in case we should all be burned in our beds. How my dad thought the sun might shine so brilliantly at night I never questioned. Not that it mattered: I never fully understood the difference between concave and convex anyway, and arbitrarily divided the lenses into the ones I liked the shape of and those I didn't. And the place never burned down.

Eventually my father had a young girl come in, and the presentation and care of the glasses became more elaborate, even baffling. She produced rolls of a material which she called chamois, but which wasn't to be found in any dictionary I examined. We used it to wrap the glasses for protection—a move which I felt was not gentle to the sensitivities of our customers. Heavy or dirty objects were forbidden in the area used for preparing new frames, and she had the walls decorated with black and white pictures of girls wearing ornate and ugly 'high-fangled specs' which she claimed were all the rage. And she even stayed late once in a while to touch up the pictures with crayon so they looked all modern and special.

But the task of cleaning the lenses, the delicate things now kept under the counter—that important task remained mine.

By this time many people began to insist on some form of examination before parting with their money, so my dad asked around and eventually came up with one of those letter charts—big letters on top, small letters subordinate. It was the only parable he used.

After a time he got to enjoy his endless pacing back and forth in front of that chart (sometimes with a pointer in his hand!), tut-tutting at each error or hesitation, which was, of course, designed to throw the customer-stroke-patient into a wild panic where only the best glasses would suffice. Though, of course, he was too kind a man and too generous with his sympathies to allow an ageing neighbour to depart distraught.

'A cup of hot tea. The only cure.'

Nevertheless, the shoe box of old reliables remained under the counter for those older members of society who preferred to trust their own judgement in the matter of selection, and leave scientific advances to the next generation. Perhaps it wasn't possible to see the Dublin they knew through the modern lenses....

Standing before the window, I watched the reflection of the labourers grouped around their stove as if it were the middle of winter. In the corner of the window I could see the wrecking ball, the bull-dozers, the trucks waiting to carry the rubble away. But, more importantly, I felt the window was watching all of this, too. I felt the desire to go inside and look out, to see the world again from its perspective.

By the time my father passed on, the area was already in decline and, though both events were in most ways unconnected, they seemed together to herald somehow the end of an era. Slowly things vanished; neighbours moved off; the bus stops in the street were re-arranged to make way for the expected increase in traffic. Old buildings came down in clouds of dust; sometimes new, concrete things went up in their places, sometimes nothing—empty spaces guarded by hoardings, splattered with rock concert posters or pictures of smiling politicians, their lips touched up to tantalize babies.

The eye looked out on a town disfigured, a street with its teeth kicked in.

'Four o'clock,' said the foreman.

I used to get home from school about now, dash across the street into the doorway, tidy my hair, chuck my satchel into the cupboard and begin polishing glasses, polish until tea-time.

Carefully I put my hand on the door handle. It felt strange to be reaching down. The door opened like the lid of an old school desk. I went in, closing it behind me, shutting the present outside. The floorboards had rotted. I could taste sherbet on my lips. My father's three-legged stool lay on its broken back. Jewels of spectacle glass winked in the dusty spotlights of boarded side windows. Under the counter I found the shoe box, exactly where it had always been, now full of skeletal remains and broken glass, the epitaph 'spectacles' on the side in my father's clumsy script, faded by years—my years away from Dublin, of not stopping long enough to remember.

I had forgotten the pictures of the ladies which could stand unsupported on the counter. Perhaps they had been put there during my father's period of illness when the business had started to fall apart unsupervised.

A car pulled up outside and I went to the window.

The youngest labourer was pointing to his watch.

'Four o'clock,' he mouthed.

Someone who appeared to be important walked over to where the workmen were relaxing. They pointed to the window and dug their heels into the gravel. The foreman bit his lip. Others of them spat.

I didn't have much time.

Down in the bottom of the window I noticed a pair of black-framed glasses, their arms folded almost in waiting. Under a constant drip one lens was clear, the other an opaque grey—a piece of slate. My father would stand at that window, his hands clasped behind his back, bobbing up and down on his toes, so that his head always moved but his tan-coloured shopcoat hung motionless around him. He always had his bi-focals (which he didn't need) perched down on the end of a nose which he likened to Agatha Christie stories—'finely crafted with a sudden twist on the end'. I'd look up his long face and find his eyebrows magnified into wild bushes while his eyes might appear like tiny green peas. Sometimes he'd jab a hand into my hair, point to the shoe box, and I'd slouch over to the counter, pretending to be his prisoner. He'd stamp his heels like an angry captor, and then, if someone came, in he'd look totally confused as he tried to remember how he should behave as an optician. I'd drag my feet around trying to make him laugh as he magnified people's eyes so that they looked like giant insects in his darkened laboratory.

I took the glasses from the window, and wiped the grey lens on my sleeve until, still semi-clouded, the world appeared like a daguerreotype, the edges of vision fading off to a blur. The men were still talking, some of them smoking, the new arrival with his hands folded high across his chest. Like the glasses. Behind them was a tower of as-yet empty offices whose mirrored windows reflected the chaos of the street, threw back the image in rejection. The reflections made the new building almost invisible in the wilderness of rafters and rubble.

The top of the shop counter was made of a substance I used to call 'Moonstone'. It seemed to be formed by green crystals, like slab of coloured ice, except that it was not particularly cold to touch. Around the edge was a band of metal which held the Moonstone in place. The corners of it were buckled into little lips on which we often snagged our clothes, and sometimes our fingers.

I lightly made a fingerprint in the dust. It looked as though the finger had been there for years, and was being lifted only now to reveal this tiny green island in a sea of ageing. And in a way it *had* been there all those years, and I wasn't so much revisiting as leaving home for the first time.

I opened the door.

A football sped down the street, bouncing along the footpath with me in pursuit, so that sometimes I went left and it went right, the two of us like characters from the musical *Oliver,* dashing through the school-children, past the coloured shopfronts, the polished brass of hall doors, women pushing prams, girls skipping, someone sweeping the footpath outside his house, old Abraham collecting scrap metal in his little pram, until, with some fancy footwork, I trapped it and brought it back to our game at the other end of the street where a cigarette break had been called in my absence.

Standing there in the doorway, I saw myself as a boy with a ball dash past....

The daylight dazzled me a little. The workmen were already standing by their machines like racing drivers. One or two even had coloured hard-hats on. A group of young children tossed stones about in idle expectation.

An ice-cream jingled by, heading for the new suburbs.

They watched it go.

And a woman pointed, holding her toddler by the hand as he strained to reach a muddy puddle with his lollipop.

The machines moved, inched forward, gravel whizzing from their tracks in all directions, ringing off the stacks of scrap-metal fittings and corrugated iron— 'luvly bits of metal' old Abraham would drag away to his little flat off South Circular Road—if he were still around.

I shut the door behind me, walked past the schoolkids who thought they were seeing a ghost appear from the condemned building.

Labourers stood about, spitting and nodding to one another through the dust, as if they planned to attack in rehearsed formation.

The taxi I had come in was still parked in the same spot, the driver stripped to his string vest, leaning against the bonnet of his old Anglia and licking an ice-cream which, through no provocation of mine, he explained he had bought when an ice-cream van had to stop to avoid hitting a chicken.

'No, no, honest to Jaysus, a chicken. Strolling across the road.'

I sat in to his car. With a gulp he had finished his ice-cream.

In the wing mirror everything looked small. It was like sitting there watching television, the same feeling of distance. The engine started somewhere behind us. I turned to see the big ball take aim, swing back and punch its first great hole in the walls. Rafters groaned, glass shattered; the big eye-window tumbled in on itself. The building squinted, briefly. And the street went blind.

BIRTH OF AN HISTORIAN

Wednesdays irritated Flynn: he could not console himself that the week was half over, but despaired instead that there was still half to go.

However, this Wednesday was different. He had arrived early for class in his customary brown, baggy suit. Puffing on his cigarette, he waited outside the door until the bell rang and the Latin teacher, Hobby Horse Dobson, came scurrying out with his head down.

'Morning'—a grunt. Well, perhaps not all that different.

'Eh, morning,' Flynn said, caught slightly unawares as he searched for a hole in the wood-panelled walls where he could extinguish his butt—walls which leaned so much with age they gave the dim corridor the appearance of a street snaking through the ruins of a city. He crossed the room, still exhaling the last of the smoke in a long and even stream, placed his books on the desk and lazily began to rub away the remainder of the Latin from the blackboard with a piece of discoloured rag. Chalk dust swirled in a single beam of sunlight as he wrote the word 'Cromwell' across the variously-shaded grey.

In the corridor the running and shouting of boys gradually faded.

'OK, where was he born?'

'Huntingdon, sir.'

'And where did he die?'

'Whitehall, sir'—the answers to all the questions so obviously concealed in minute script on the covers of jotters or along the spines of text-books that Kevin Byrne couldn't help feeling that Flynn was just as responsible for the whole charade as were the boys in his care. Not that Kevin cared! Whatever system the teacher and class worked out between themselves was fine by him—just so long as he was expected to have no part of it.

Already the last morning of school had begun—much like any other—Flynn wandering the aisles between desks, counting the minutes to his 11 o'clock cigarette break, rehearsing the jokes he had heard the previous evening for the day's debut in the Teachers Room.

Kevin scratched his head and sank into another of his regular daydreams.

'Good morning, Mr Cromwell,' said the birds of the morning, twittering in the tree tops.

Cromwell put down Raleigh's weighty History of the World *and stretched himself.*

'Already...' he said, abstracted, running a rough hand through his auburn hair.

'Find me someone who can write,' he called out. 'And where's my breakfast?'

Over at the Rock of Dunamase the sun was bringing daylight to the castle's occupants—a shepherd or two, boys with buckets of water, soldiers slumped against the stout, stone walls. A girl with a sheet of bright red hair scrubbed a frockcoat in slightly dirty water.

A young man came and stood uneasily in front of Cromwell.

'Mr Lely,' Cromwell suddenly began his letter, fingering the great mole beneath his lower lip and eyeing the boy with suspicion. 'I desire you would use all your skill to paint my picture truly like me, and not flatter me at all; but remark all these roughnesses, pimples, warts and everything as you see me, otherwise...' and he grimaced, 'I never will pay a farthing for it.'

The young man scribbled in a wild longhand, struggling to keep pace and, when he'd finished, Cromwell took the letter for inspection and dismissed him with a wave of his hand.

He amused himself a while with this private joke. Then someone arrived carrying a rabbit breakfast.

For four years Kevin had kept himself entertained, directing wild films in his head with the plots provided by the day's history lesson. And once his latest film had gone into production, he had a distant look in his eyes that separated him from his classmates as surely as if he had hung a 'Do Not Disturb' sign about his neck.

At break-time, while all the other boys slapped punctured handballs against the bicycle shed wall, or secretly puffed cigarettes in its corners, Kevin would slouch with a silent friend or two at the least-frequented end of the playing yard, recounting his histories to anyone who cared to listen.

However, most of the time, as now, when he found himself trapped in the classroom, he made sure to sit boldly up front while Flynn strained to keep watch on those at the back who were trying to be inconspicuous.

Today he found himself in the middle of what he considered the most important part of the whole course, an event so special it had been saved for this, the final day.

The two colonels came riding from opposite directions, long feathers protruding from their colourful hats.

'Ah, John,' said Sir John Reynolds.

'Hello,' said Colonel Hewson, grinning. 'Anything planned for today?'

'Not really. I thought I might just wander about, see if the Irish are behaving themselves.'

'Mind if I come along... for company?' said Hewson, sensing some fun ahead.

'Be my guest,' replied Reynolds, affecting a low curtsey.

And off they rode, Hewson on a white horse, Reynolds on a dappled pony whose ear had been bitten off in a skirmish outside Dublin with some wild-looking Irish, drunk on potato wine.

Off they rode through the bog, their horses labouring in the damp peat.

Off they rode, cat-calling to peasant girls who hid behind furze bushes at their approach.

Off they rode—comfortable—while their huge army of press-ganged illiterates trudged along behind the swishing tails of their mounts, pulling metal cannon that squelched through the mud or made sparks where they crossed stoney paths.

Off they rode, Cromwell's two giddy colonels, looking for some game to play in the frustrating silence of the midland countryside.

There was only one way to ring a bell. The tall, reed-like Christian Brother known as Stork knew that it was with violence. He was built like a sailor and dressed like a nun. After twelve years in the school he had discovered only recently that his nickname did not refer to his physical stature but to his rumoured weakness for bringing little boys close to his mouth. And so now, as well as with his ordinary, everyday, fervour, he shook the bell with rage, all the rage in his brittle arms. The younger boys stopped immediately what they were doing and ran to the school doors to form two neat lines in an instant. The older ones dragged their sneakers across the roughly-lain tarmac in front of the statue of Edmund Rice, a resolute group still huddled in the bicycle-shed corner. The silent Stork walked back towards the school, one hand up inside the bell to prevent its ringing, a spear-like shadow moving towards the monastic gloom.

And all that remained to confirm that the year had passed was the final speech, to which no one would listen.

In the meantime, however, the day dragged on. And while Hobby Horse Dobson enthused in his booming voice next door about the poetry of Virgil, and Flynn flicked through notes to remind himself of the dates of Queen Elizabeth, the captivating sound of girls playing in the nearby convent school silenced the normally unruly classroom; and for fifteen minutes they listened lonely as clouds to the heavenly chorus, while Dobson, worked up to a lather of perspiration, hauled the enormous horse inside the walls.

Cromwell ate his breakfast with little heart, having been up all the previous night, unable to sleep in the cold sweat of an ague. To console himself he had read some more from Raleigh's comprehensive masterpiece. He also wondered occasionally about Hewson and Reynolds.

'Byrne!' Flynn was shouting. 'Answer the question.'
'Sir?'
'The significance of the date on which Oliver Cromwell entered Sidney Sussex College in Cambridge, if you please.'
Kevin's mind went blank.
'Shakespeare,' whispered a voice behind him.
'Shakespeare, sir.' He guessed: 'Shakespeare died, sir.'
Flynn spun expertly on one heel and resumed reading aloud from the text.

Hewson and Reynolds had arrived in a small wooded valley, and could see Dunamase castle silhouetted on top of a hill. It didn't look particularly impressive: good strong-looking walls, certainly, but the grass around the place wasn't kept neat the way it would have been back in Oxfordshire.

Hewson dismounted slowly and motioned that his horse be looked after. He was obviously thinking about something because he had long since ceased the singing of nursery rhymes with bawdy endings, which were often his sole form of communication while travelling. He sat up on a felled tree, looking up at the grinning face of Reynolds and tapping a stubby, ringed finger rhythmically on his pouted lips.

'H'mm. What do you think?'

'Oh, let's,' said Reynolds, understanding the implication. 'This place is so boring.'

Hewson thought about it some more and frowned in the direction of the castle. Suddenly he stood.

'Right,' he said, clapping his hands softly like a man who has agreed to carve the Sunday joint. 'Right. Right.'

Soldiers darted in all directions, the stronger ones taking on the job of assembling and preparing the big cannon, the others fanning out under cover of tall trees. Hewson and Reynolds moved out of the way to talk about their adventures in the Army Mutinies and the archery lessons they had had back in Oxfordshire.

Finally, when everything was ready, Hewson took a burning taper, looked at it for a moment, and handed it back to a soldier who in moments had launched the first metal ball at the castle. With the loud thump shepherds fled for cover, while soldiers dashed for gates and parapets. Huge stones fell on heads and bones. The roofs first and, one by one, the stone walls shuddered and collapsed in the sun. Soon, little more than a cloud of dust could be seen on the once fortified hilltop.

However, once the third or fourth ball had been fired, the cannon had begun to lose their novelty for Hewson and Reynolds who decided to move on with their exhausted entourage, Reynolds announcing his intention of riding side-saddle for a change.

When the bell finally came it still managed to make some of them jump. Stork was being as violent as his recent realization had been bitter. He was further angered by having to be the bearer of the present good news of liberation. The boys imagined him eyeing his long-treasured bell with disgust—if they pictured him at all; because, all of a sudden, schoolbags had been packed and they were charging for the door and pouring out into the corridor, shoving each other aside and rapping on the doors of classes not yet liberated.

Flynn threw his feet up on the desk and lit himself a cigarette. It was a day for breaking rules.

'What the hell.... Want one?' he said to Kevin. Kevin put his hand out.

'Thanks.' He slipped the gift into his pocket and left.

A breeze played in the long grass on the ruin. Kevin stood watching it, trying to catch his breath after the steep climb and against the wind that raced over the top of the hill. He let his bicycle fall into the support of a thorn bush. Then he climbed the rough steps at the entrance to the castle. The breeze ran right along the top of the largest remaining piece of wall, over slabs of stone where arches or spiral stairs may once have stood. He looked out over the valley, trying to imagine Hewson and Reynolds among the trees, swapping stories, Reynolds clapping his hands and throwing back his head in laughter.

Taking out a school jotter and leaving it open beside him, he shut his eyes to the castle that history had left unfinished.

At first he could see nothing—blackness. Then, gradually, shapes began to appear: horses, feathers, cannon being dragged through mud. He heard the axles squeak, the soldiers curse under their breaths. He pulled back the lens of his vision and saw local children clutching their chickens to them, holding mothers and old men tightly about the thighs and knees, pictures not unlike the children he knew from newspaper reports of war-torn lands.

He pulled back further and saw his own familiar landscape before him, but without roads, without concrete, without the fingerprints of his century upon it.

And then Cromwell, sitting up with his favourite book until dawn, intrigued by the exploits of the Trojans.

And Hewson, a little drunk, confessing to Reynolds that he'd been conferred with an honorary Master of Arts without so much as having glimpsed a single book in twenty years.

THE SENTENCE
(OR THE BEST THING ABOUT LIVING
SEVEN FLOORS UP)

The best thing about living seven floors up is we don't get mice.

'Blast!' What kind of way was that to begin a letter home? Her first in weeks. Her parents would believe she'd finally gone mad. They might even ring that fat man next door—again. Had she really once been so naïve as to have given them the number of a total stranger in case of emergency? How had she put the question to him originally? 'I don't have a phone and my parents in Ireland might be worried about my sanity'? And had he really consented, that little man who watched football all day with the sound up full, that little man who no longer even bothered to grunt when she passed him on the stairs. No, she couldn't bear to have him knock on her door and give her that 'just-who-do-you-Irish-think-you-are' look, couldn't bear to talk to her mother again surrounded by that little man's football paraphernalia and iconography.

She would have to write.

But what was there to say? 'I'm fine. London's a great place. The guy next door is really friendly'?

The best thing... She looked at that strange sentence she had written, and then down the blank page before her. One sentence in almost two months. Two words and a full stop.

But at least it's the truth, she thought. At least it's not a lie like the silence I hope they will interpret as: no news is good news. That silence had outgrown even her mother's optimism. She could no longer continue to send it home like a blank letter. 'No news is good news. I'm fine. London's a great place.'

She thought a while longer, but went back to bed when the sentence refused company.

About six o'clock the biscuit-tin lid on the wall clanged. She sat up in bed and watched it jerk about on the string, striking the rough plaster. The photograph of tubular chimes she had cut from a magazine and pasted over it did little to amuse her now. He was home.

She climbed from beneath the warm blankets, stepped over the previous day's dinner plates, and started towards the hallway.

'Hurry up,' he called irritably. She could hear rain, the biscuit-tin lid jumping violently.

Her shirt! She tried to remember where she'd left it earlier. He never liked to see her walk about the flat without it on, didn't even like her partial nudity—not unless he had first made advances towards her, had sat up on the arm of her chair in his own good time and slipped his hand into her trouser waist, or pushed himself against her behind as she washed up in the kitchen. On such occasions he would insist on her nudity. He might instruct her to strip, to stand before him, to walk about then while he just sat there, usually smoking.

Then he felt he could control her nakedness and, therefore, he was no longer threatened by it. His fear would have been passed over to her, and she would accept it, for peace' sake.

What she did not do for peace....

But where *was* her shirt?

She decided to pull a blanket from the bed and, wrapping it about her, ran to the door in her bare feet.

'What the hell is going on in there?' He pushed by her and into the living room. She shut the door with her behind, leaning against the coldness for a moment.

'Well...'

She saw his hand reach for the television switch.

'What are you doing out there? Why don't you have any clothes on?' He looked up at her from his chair. He'd already taken off his shoes and was unbuckling the belt of his pants to relieve his spreading belly.

Her arms were folded across her chest. 'I've had...'

'What? A Shower? Without getting your hair wet?'

'I...'

'Your clothes.' He threw her shirt across the room. She picked it up and went back into the hallway. She could hear him stand, turn up the television and sit back down on the bed. He would feel her warmth still there.

She peeped back in.

'Yes?'

'Would you like some tea?'

'Clothes are good enough for everyone else!' he shouted.

He was sitting in his chair, away from the bed. She sighed, went back into the hallway and dressed.

The best thing about living seven floors up is we don't get mice.

She looked at the sentence, tried to imagine her mother reading it:

'That's all?'

'That's all she says, Frank. 'The best thing about living..."

'Here, let me see.' Her father would want to examine the thing more closely. He would probably spend as much time trying to puzzle it out as she had spent these last few days in its writing. He would sit up with it all night, poring over it, wondering if it hadn't been written under the influence of drink—drugs, even; he understood there were pressures on young people nowadays, things he had never encountered in his youth. He would try his best to find something hidden in the sentence, something his wife could never hope to find at her self-imposed distance from reality. He would attempt to decipher it the way he had once deciphered codes during the war—a military fanatic marooned in a neutral country.

First of all, he would examine it for sexual innuendo, for a phrase that sparked off some memory from her childhood (though that period could hardly be said to be over yet), for some reference that only he might understand. Then, of course, he would be forced to sit and drink coffee, blaming himself when all he could succeed in seeing in her one and only letter in two months was a simple statement concerning mice. Susan could see her father at home in the kitchen, re-writing the sentence, struggling to find meaning in it read backwards, phonetically, jumbled up, even making anagrams from it, and finally falling asleep over it until her mother would come down in the morning, still in her pink nightdress, having just discovered the uncreased pillow beside her:

'Frank?'

'Mice,' her husband would shrug.

He lay on the bed behind her, snoring. There seemed little chance of his waking as he almost always slept soundly, stubbornly even. But if he should have happened to wake—and probably for sexual reasons—she could always have slipped the sheet of paper into her open bag by the side of the bed. It was the only place where she knew she would be beyond the reach of his hands and eyes—there among the creams, aerosols and tampons.

The best thing...

Even as a single sentence she knew it was flawed. Get mice? She hadn't meant they didn't *get* mice—from a shop or something. She'd meant they didn't have a mouse problem, a problem with mice. She knew she should begin again, make it 'have', 'we don't *have* mice'. If only one sentence were to be sent home by her, it ought to be correct at least.

But by now she was beginning to see the sentence in the same way that she had once seen the body of love poems in her old school jotters: imperfect though it was she could not bring herself to change a single word. It would be like betraying the person she had been. Now the sentence had begun to exhibit a will of its own, it had a purpose and reason beyond her. And yet she knew it was ridiculous to expect her parents to make any sense of it—to read between the line, as it were.

Is it a thread from my unravelling mind? A washing line from which hangs a spotless sheet?

In this mood she played with the idea of a haiku—

The best thing about
living seven floors up is
we don't get mice

—but found she was a syllable short, so she got up and went to the kitchen.

The kitchen was a greasy affair, without hot water or proper ventilation. The windows remained boarded up as they had been found a year previously, in case the shabbiness of the interior of the flat might attract other prospective squatters. Only from the bedroom was there any 'view' as such—the boarded kitchen windows of Kemble House, the next in a chain of run-down buildings that seemed to shackle her like a prisoner to this god-forsaken place.

The best thing... Certainly there was no one worst thing she could think of.

Unless her name. 'Write home, Suzie. We worry.' She hated when her mother called her that. It was a doll's name, a blonde doll with a snub nose and sexy, plastic legs. It was the name of the girl who found herself living with a dirty Irishman in a barely-furnished squat in London. It was the name *he* liked to call her, he who treated her the way he had once treated his younger sister's dolls, ignoring them during the day but all curious after they had been tucked away for the night.

But it was not *her* name. *Her* name was Sue. *They* could call her what they liked. It did not change her name.

The best thing about living seven floors up is we don't get mice. Sue.

Wasn't that it? At last her sentence had the extra syllable she had needed.

But somehow she was no longer interested in poetry.

She stirred her coffee with a greasy spoon and saw the bare lightbulb reflect on all the tiny globules. She stirred again and again and, though the little galaxy of reflections whirled round and round, it always came to a halt as if confronting her with something.

Over in the corner, one of the bulging refuse sacks slid a little against the stained wall.

Her name, the squat, him, his beer cans always accumulating around the floor, the little fat man next door, the old men and women curling up in the doorways of the Underground, the Alsatians that were forever sniffing around the urine-smelling elevators.... No, there was certainly no one worst thing.

Standing, she took a mouthful from her coffee and emptied the remainder down the sink, careful to rinse out the cup as was her habit.

The best thing...

She lifted the page that had been sitting before her on the table, folded it neatly, slipped it into the envelope already addressed.

He was snoring loudly in the other room. She placed the envelope between the full ashtray and an empty beer can on the up-turned tea-chest beside the bed. That would be the first place he would look in the morning, reaching for a cigarette butt and shaking the can in desperation.

Seeing her shirt on the back of a chair, she bent instinctively to put it on, but changed her mind and left it where it was.

She drew back the bolt and opened the front door.

A night train passed in the distance.

The best thing...

Stepping out, oblivious to the cold, she could have sworn she saw tiny eyes peep from behind a discarded crisp bag and disappear

Strange Bedfellows

The Kavanagh brothers had not spoken to each other in years. Twenty? Thirty? How many was not important. Neither could the number have been agreed upon had they deigned to discuss it. One may suppose that they had long since ceased to ask themselves such questions. In their isolated cottage their visitors were few. They visited no one. What friends they'd had years before, they no longer knew to be alive or dead. And, anyway, they might have argued, what would have been the use of such protracted communication? At their ages there remained only one thing to which either brother might devote such energies—a thing to do with land. And, as time passed, that one thing seemed to move ever further out of reach. Instead the brothers occupied themselves with their respective monologues and silences.

The fact of the matter was that neither of the Kavanaghs—now 65 and 69 years respectively—could have calculated his own or his brother's age with anything approaching certainty. Perhaps it was that the trees which ringed their dilapidated cottage had somehow managed to keep time outside. Indeed, whenever he allowed himself to think about it, Michael, the younger of the two, was given to such fancy notions. Certainly it was difficult to explain in conventional terms.

Either way the most they knew was that Tom was the elder and that Michael's blindness meant he would probably prove the least resilient of the two, that is, that he would be the first to crack under the strain. Then, finally, the game would end and the farm would belong to Tom.

In secret, that must have been the conclusion to which each of them inevitably came. But the game was far from ending.

How much of the day they actually spent under the shadow of regret one can not be certain, but even with nothing happening there was much to do. That they were still alive in the same three-roomed cottage in which they had been raised must also have been some consolation. And even if they were too old or stubborn to busy themselves with making much-needed repairs to the ancestral home, the thought of same must have occupied at least some of their hours. Questions of time they would scarcely have found time to consider. Arthritis now caused them more concern than did amnesia. And the miraculous arrival of Meals on Wheels and boy scout window-washers from the outside world was evidence enough to conclude that such an outside world must still exist and would be there for the one who proved the most enduring. For, as the Kavanaghs knew, endurance was everything.

Occupying a sort of twilight zone—neither child- nor adult-hood—from their cottage by the side of the road, if ever they did glimpse the world outside they were not affected by it. There in their parents' house where their mother, already a lifetime dead, still watched over them, things were remembered where they had not stood for years.

And if their father, old Mr Kavanagh, had really died in 1926, he was no less vehement with trespassers when he visited Tom in dreams to recommend the use of buckshot. In the Kavanagh household the past and present, like the aged brothers themselves, made strange bedfellows. While Tom, in a litany of complaints to a passing stranger, might see his sightless brother damned in hell over some childhood difference of opinion, Michael might describe the groans of a woman heard in his brother's bedroom more than twenty years before as if it had happened that very morning. At any moment the talk might turn to the Eucharistic Congress or VE Day, and either one might begin to expound the merits of Nazism or the qualities of Hitler in a voice uncannily like that of his dead father. These opinions, though they were inevitably overheard, were never directed from one brother to the other.

And yet, though their enforced proximity was by times enough to bring them close to violence, when they were out of each other's way neither could be content with his new found freedom. Michael rummaged around in the kitchen or in the front garden wondering what it was that Tom was up to in the fields. Could he have been all the time selling the farm off piece by piece? What had happened to the chair that since father's time had been here in this corner? Tom, meanwhile, suspected that his brother's blindness might have been compensated for by a miraculous improvement in hearing. As well as removing his boots when he was at home, he took to engaging in imaginary conversations while in the fields or on the road, in case his house-bound brother might be listening. As local parlance had it, there was a pair of them in it.

Like many conflicts, and family conflicts in particular, the one which occupied the Kavanagh brothers had its origins in a land dispute. When their father passed away without a will, the two young sons took on the task of maintaining the farm. But shortly after their mother's death an accident which left Michael blind in middle-age made it clear to Tom that he would never make the place amount to anything, so long as he carried the responsibility of caring for another. His initial enthusiasm waned to endurance, and the conflict began. Tom refused to lift a hand to anything and spent less and less time about the place. Stories reached Michael about his brother's carousing, and when the two found themselves together their exchanges were far from being constructive. Before long the neglected farm was out of control and the brothers were exhausted by their arguments.

And so, knowing neither one could win or lose, they settled down for the long siege—a brother in either bedroom, and weeds cracking flagstones in the yard. The back door, which once opened out onto a cluster of outhouses, was now nailed up so overgrown had the rear of the dwelling become. Rats ran freely through the empty barn and a tree lay inches from the cottage where it had fallen ten or fifteen winters before.

Michael, being blind, could venture less far than his brother, and was forced to pass much of his time in the few square yards in front of the house and before the road. And even here there were unpulled nails in planks and skeins of wire about the place. Tom regularly ventured down back lanes or into fields where Michael's disability prevented him from going. Only there could he feel outside of the range of his brother's hearing.

The locals, who had by now mythologized the brothers' obstinacy, would choose alternative, longer routes to town to avoid taking sides or being implicated in the brothers' feud. In fact the only regular visitors to the cottage were members of the local charities who brought a hot meal to the brothers every day about noon. And even so they were seldom invited to cross the Kavanagh threshold.

As well as being half washed away by flooding streams and riddled with pot-holes, the road which passed the cottage went nowhere in particular. Once over the hills, which it seemed to climb with reluctance, it faded away to little more than a dirt track with a ridge of grass growing down the centre. The outlying farms once served by it now joined up to a main road on the other side over which heavy farm machinery could gain access. Perhaps at some stage in the future the quiet road would accommodate a line of modern bungalows in an ideal environment in which to raise children. But for the present, the Kavanaghs were, insofar as it is possible, cut off from the world.

Angela stood by the roadside. If she was not altogether oblivious to the water running down her neck, her feet were too tired and sore for her to care. She had no real idea where she was, nor did she know where she was going. She knew only that she had to get away from her father and mother, from her school and the threat of final examinations. She knew that she would recognize her destination when, and if, she found it. It would be a quiet place where no one would know her and she could re-invent herself. She had about £30 in her pocket and, despite having wandered for two days, knew she was not far from home.

Michael lay in bed, listening to his stomach growl. Why was it that they only came on alternate days, or sometimes only twice a week? he asked himself. Did that outside world, whatever it was like, really believe he could exist on so little nourishment? Was it any surprise that when the weather got cold he had to take to bed?

When he had put these questions to the doctor some days earlier, he had been assured that his mind was playing tricks on him. The doctor had personally checked to see that the brothers were not being forgotten by the organizers of the run, and that regular deliveries of food were continuing to the Kavanagh place, even when the floods or snows had made the roads all but impassable. It was nothing more, the doctor had been sure, than a falling off of memory on Michael's part. He had even suggested a small vitamin supplement....

Michael, however, had remained unconvinced, and swore to keep a track of things. Even his fool-proof system of placing a match-stick in a box—to represent each meal received—let him down when he twice forgot he had initiated the system and began again. The doctor had found three boxes with a total of 18 match-sticks on his return after only a week. His solution had been to increase the supplement.

Though the doctor had not noticed, nor could Michael Kavanagh have seen, the calendar in his bedroom was the last one bought by Mrs Kavanagh the Christmas before she died. Unturned, the page of the month of her death, in the year of her death, was the only thing on the wall in what once had been her bedroom and was now her son's.

'Don't you worry, Mr Kavanagh. You're just a little tired. That's all,' said the doctor. What was the chill he had felt in the cluttered room? He patted himself with feigned good humour on the stomach.

'Now if you had a paunch like this you might have cause for concern.'

Michael had brightened, but waned again as if he had not really understood the joke. He listened to the doctor's fumbling with his bag, torn between a respect for the profession and a distrust of the man. As far as he was concerned (whatever any doctor might have said), something was definitely wrong.

Kavanagh lay there, trying to puzzle it out (Had the meeting occurred earlier that day, or the day before?), when he heard someone at the door. He climbed stiffly out of bed and went to the kitchen.

Maybe this was them now. What day was today? He rubbed his bristled neck, felt something hard, picked at it.

He put a hand to the kettle on the range and found it piping hot—a sign that Tom had not recently refilled it after making tea. He concluded therefore that he was alone, that Tom was somewhere on his wanderings.

The tap dripped into a basin. He turned in the middle of the room. Had the kettle been hot or cold just now? He could not remember.

'Anybody home?' Angela rapped the door. Something metallic clanged about inside. Suddenly Michael was in the doorway in his stained long-johns and stockinged feet, peering through her. Confronted by him, Angela realized that she had not decided what it was she had wanted. The rain had eased off and it seemed ridiculous now that the storm had ended to be seeking shelter. The realization left her looking for something to say as she stood before the blind man in his underwear.

'Are you going into town?' he said. 'Cos if you are, the bastards have left me without a crust—again! Ah, I might as well be talking to the wall.'

He shut the door before she could reply.

When the rain stopped, she left the take-away in town to walk around. She was dry now and had managed to change her socks in the toilet. Already it was evening. She stood in the square looking up and down but saw no sign of life other than a flashing neon sign outside a pub. With nowhere else to go she spent until closing time inside and then went back to her B&B where the landlady complained about the time. Angela went to bed feeling cold and alone. At £7.50 per night, and with her mother and father presumably worried about her, she knew it would not be long before she would have to go back.

The following morning she listened to the birds in the tree outside her window. She couldn't remember the last time she'd heard so inviting a sound and, skipping breakfast, she was up and out in the sharp sunlight. The pessimism of the previous night was a thing of the past. This, now, was a special day—not least because it would have been her first back to school after the Christmas break. She would savour every breath of it.

All along the street there was movement. School children held hands at the corner waiting for a tractor to pass and, if not in that moment, then in the hours that followed, she decided to spend the last of her time and money here, to see what would happen.

Somehow the little country town seemed infinitely more exciting than her own which she had left just days before, vowing to escape its monotony. Here, though she might not fit in, she could at least feel different until she was ready to return.

She ate that day in the same restaurant she had visited the night before, and it pleased her that already she could detect signs of curiosity from the locals. The proprietor spoke with a thick country accent when he greeted her with 'How's it going?' and took her order. It was difficult to decide if he expected a reply. She had two breakfast specials and drank coffee in a window seat until noon. Then she took a walk.

As she was passing the supermarket on her tour of town she thought of the old man in the doorway the evening before. What did he mean about being 'without a crust'? She thought about him as she sat on a bench outside the church watching two men carry out a statue of an ox. A minute later she was in the supermarket, buying bread and milk and a tin of soup.

As she approached the cottage she could hear the sound of wood being chopped inside. She opened the gate and walked up the unweeded path.

'What is it you want?' said Tom, standing in the door with a hatchet in his hand.

'I was looking... I was looking for... the blind fellow,' said Angela.

'Ha.' This second old fellow threw down his hatchet and sauntered past her towards the road. She stepped aside in alarm and instinctively put her hand over her face. He stood behind her defiantly.

'I have something to give him,' Angela said, holding up the groceries by way of an explanation.

'Have you now?' He considered it. 'I'll see to those.'

'I'd rather give him them myself.'

Tom grinned and pointed in the direction of the cottage. Angela went to the door.

The room was dark even though a bare lightbulb burned in a lamp above the table. She dared not venture any further than where she stood. Tom watched her from the gate.

'Is anybody home?'

To her left a door began to open, and the man she had seen the previous day appeared. His face was an unearthly white and was patched with two scraps of bloodied toilet paper.

'What is it? What have you got?' he said, abruptly.

She offered the bag, touching it against his arm so that he might find it.

'Just bread and stuff....'

'Bread! You're joking!' He jerked violently. 'No effin' meat?'

'There's oxtail soup.'

'No effin' meat?' He stiffened. 'You tell them they're a pack of bastards. You tell them I said... Who pays the taxes? That's what I want to know. '

He cleared his throat, which brought on a fit of coughing and forced him to hold the door frame for support.

Angela put the bag down at his feet and retreated from the gloomy kitchen. Whatever about her initial idea of having a chat with him, she thought it far better now to get out of his way.

Michael leaned against the door-post and seemed not to notice that she was leaving.

As she was going out the gate, Tom came close to her and teased. 'Man does not live on bread alone.' And he produced a set of false teeth from his pocket, chomped them in the air and stuck them into his mouth.

In the doorway his brother, who had by now opened the bag, held the tin of soup above his head and called:

'The effers think I'm going to open this?'

He threw the tin into the grass and slammed the door.

Tom stood laughing by the gate and she felt his eyes on her until she had rounded the bend in the road.

What were these people talking about? What was going on there? Had the blind one mistaken her for someone else? She noticed her excitement but refused to put it down to fear.

The car sounded its horn though it was still a good distance away from her and was travelling slowly. The middle-aged woman waved to her as she passed, and then rounded the bend in the direction of the Kavanagh place. A moment later Angela heard the car stop and she guessed that the woman had gone to see the old fellows. She could hear that the engine had been left running. She paused for a minute and thought she heard voices, but she couldn't make out what it was they said. Then she heard the car door close, the engine switch to a harsher sound and the car reappeared heading back towards town.

'Can I give you a lift?' said the driver, slowing almost to a halt alongside her.

Angela hesitated.

'Come on.' The middle-aged woman opened the door and Angela jumped in.

'Friends of yours?' said the woman, presently. She was dressed like royalty—a fur coat, a hat with a brooch.

'No,' said Angela. 'I mean, not really.'

'Good,' said the woman. 'Barmy old boys, the same pair.'

Angela laughed. She liked the way the woman had said 'barmy', the Englishy accent. A Protestant, she supposed, and wondered what her mother would say.

Almost with a start she noticed the smell of food around her and, looking back over the seat, saw all sorts of pots and plates and cardboard boxes.

'Oh that,' said the woman, anticipating her question. 'Meals on Wheels, you know. We must all do our bit.'

Her passenger smiled.

Whatever was still holding her there, Angela knew that it no longer had to do with feeling exotic. Only two days and already the looks and questions which she had previously taken as signs of interest seemed now the undisguised suspicion for which she hated her own town. More and more she realized that her attempt at escape was futile. She knew also that when the money ran out her feeling of independence would also disappear. To survive then she would have to look to strangers for assistance. And that would entail telling them all about herself, something she was unwilling to do. She vowed to return home in the morning and make amends with her parents. After all, the trip had been far from useless. It was still the first weeks of the year and already she had asserted herself and shown she was not to be taken for granted.

Yet, though the rain was threatening to return, and she had seen all there was to be seen, she could not leave without solving the mystery of the two old men. It was not that she particularly cared about them. In fact she could not have cared less. At home she had old neighbours and poor neighbours of her own. Her own uncle who lived nearby was not very different from either of the Kavanagh brothers, and if she had wanted to study old men she could have started with him. But Angela felt that the brothers were the one feature that would make her escapade memorable, her one significant encounter.

In the afternoon she returned to the cottage. This time Michael answered. He was more relaxed by far.

'There it is,' he said, simply, and she noticed for the first time the dark splotches of rain on her coat.

'Better come in out of that.'

She followed quietly inside.

The kitchen was heavy with the smell of urine, and, when she went to sit, she found wet blankets on the chair beneath her.

Michael stood by the range.

'The fire's dead so I can't have a cup of tea. Himself is out traipsing the fields as if they were his. I'd see him buried in them first.'

Angela tried to take in as much of this as she could, but before long Michael had had enough of her company.

'Good luck to you now,' he said, going to the door.

'Do you not want anything... in the shops?' She played for time.

Michael stopped. He frowned and twisted his head so that he was facing into the daylight.

What was it she wanted from him? she wondered.

'Get me a bottle of milk, and leave me alone. Now out, for Christ's sake!' His temper was up. Angela felt genuinely frightened.

She went to the door and Michael stepped back into the half darkness, still muttering to himself.

'I'm going,' she said, 'I'm going now,' and she shut the door so forcefully that the coat hangers on the back were almost shaken off.

But she remained in the room.

What she was doing standing there, she had no clear idea. She had certainly not planned anything of the sort. The blind Kavanagh brother stood just feet away, absolutely motionless. He seemed to be listening to everything, and she too began to listen to see what it was that he might hear. She heard the water dripping in the basin and an engine somewhere in the distance. Scarcely did she breathe herself, but she could hear his breath rasping in his scrawny chest.

Slowly Michael moved one foot slightly forward and began to test the floor beneath him. Despite her age, Angela had never really had an encounter with a blind person, let alone in a situation like this. She was fascinated. She saw him reach behind him for a stick— the first time she had seen him with one—and hold it firmly in his left hand as if he were pushing it into the ground. Her heart pounded behind her ears.

After a few moments she managed to unclench her sticky palm from around the doorknob and soundlessly let her arm fall to her side. Her legs were trembling.

Without turning, Kavanagh lowered himself into a battered armchair, all the while clinging to the stick and staring expressionlessly before him. He sat facing her but made no voluntary movement or sound.

The minutes passed. Angela was now breathing quietly and had begun counting to herself in an attempt to slow her heartbeat. Kavanagh had relaxed too and his breathing was less troubled, though he still seemed excited. She wondered how long she might escape detection, or whether he had already detected her and was simply wondering now what to do.

In an overgrown outhouse, accessible only by a back lane, his brother Tom sat eating dinner at an upturned oil-drum. A second paper plate lay empty beside his mound of sausages and mash. A crow at the empty window watched the old man try to force the huge meal down. After dinner, when Tom would be in the fields walking off his food, the crow would have the pickings for himself.

Angela was now inching her way past the window, further into the dark of the kitchen, distracting Michael's attention by tossing match-sticks across the floor. Everywhere she looked there were match-sticks. Each time one landed near him, Michael cocked his head in such a comic way that she could barely prevent herself from laughing aloud. What idiots these old men were! What absolutely idiotic behaviour! She did not know what it was but she knew that there was something going on between the pair of them.

'Who's there?' Michael sat up in the chair.

A knife teetered to the edge of the table beside her, threatening to fall, its rounded blade glinting.

'Who is it?'

The voice terrified her. Surely now she would give up the charade and take her leave. She did not know at what moment the other brother might return to find her there.

And yet the feeling of excitement, of whatever it was, would not allow her to leave. How silly Kavanagh looked! How ridiculous now that he could not shout his meaningless orders or crawl away to sulk.

Michael fingered the light stick as if he were intending to use it as a weapon and, now and again—though it may have been her imagination—he seemed to locate her with his eyes.

As he drew himself up in the armchair, she shocked both of them by suddenly stepping right up to his face and shouting 'Bastard!'

Kavanagh fell backwards with a roar. The arm of the chair broke under his weight and the chair toppled over. She heard his skull knock against the wall.

She bent to see his face. His eyes were closed, but he was breathing.

'Are you all right, you old bugge? You have a weird effect on me.'

'Piss off,' said Kavanagh. 'Put the kettle on and piss off with yourself.'

Angela left having checked that Tom was not anywhere around the front of the house. She had filled the kettle and left it to boil on the range so that Michael might brew tea when he had regained his strength. She had left a packet of chocolate biscuits in his cap on the table as a peace offering.

The meeting with the Kavanaghs had left its mark on her. Long after she had returned home—and after a near banishment from her father—she continued to wonder about them. In the beginning if she had been inclined to see them as curiosities, she now saw that they may have been normal people in an altogether abnormal situation. Though at no point was she ashamed of her behaviour with the blind one, she had not settled for an easy explanation for her actions.

That is not to say that the experience had preoccupied her afterwards. It simply struck her as strange that she had neither behaved as if she had liked the old codgers, nor as if she had wanted to steal from their house. That she ever heard about them again was a thing of chance even though her own home town was a short distance away.

The following June, her latest boyfriend arrived on his new motorcycle and was quickly surrounded by the local children. Her father was at work, and Angela, who had just completed the Leaving Certificate, was spending her afternoons watching Bogart films on television. Reluctantly she agreed to get out of the house but, after a few miles on the pillion of Mark's new bike, she was enjoying herself thoroughly and was even thinking of running off again.

While they sat with their arms around each other in a country pub—to the amusement of the locals at the bar— her eye wandered to a poster above the door.

'We're going.'

'What?' The cider made Mark contrary.

The barman had put down the television remote control and came out from behind the bar.

'You wouldn't be from around here,' he said, amicably.

'Come on. Let's go.' Angela stood up and grabbed her jacket.

'Jesus!' exclaimed Mark, with the glass still to his lips. 'We've only just sat down!'

'I want to see someone.'

The laughter continued in the bar long after they had gone.

Angela knocked and waited and knocked again. Mark straddled the bike and shook his head. The cottage looked as if it had been empty for years.

'Give it a minute.'

Mark came up behind her.

'There's obviously no one in,' he said, muffled inside the helmet. 'Are you sure it's the same place?'

Angela saw her own withering look reflected in his visor.

In town they visited the same restaurant, but this time she was ignored by the owner. Perhaps it was that she was no longer on her own.

'Do you know the Kavanaghs? Two old fellows. They have a little cottage...'

'I know them,' said the proprietor. Angela waited, but he volunteered nothing more.

'Do you know where they are?'

'Oh, come on,' said Mark. 'This is ridiculous.'

The owner sighed, as if he were sick of the story.

When the doctor had come on a casual visit a couple of months before to see how Michael was, he had found Tom at home and had shared a pot of tea with him. There had seemed nothing unusual about the place, except that the front garden looked different, somehow tidier, as if at last the brothers had decided to do a little work around the place. When he had gone into Michael's room, however, he had found him fully clothed in the bed. He had starved.

Angela left the restaurant without speaking. She was remembering the lift back to town from the Kavanagh place in the car full of food. Mark grabbed his helmet and followed her. 'So much for summer!' It was beginning to rain and neither of them had thought to bring a jacket.

PEARL

Dear Pearl,

I hope you don't think bad of me for not having written for so long. The more I postponed it, the more difficult it seemed to become, just to put pen to paper. I remember what it was they said at school, do you?—that writing was half about applying pen to paper, half about applying your backside to the seat of the chair. I might have gone on like that, in that confusion, for months yet before you would have heard a peep from me. But something's happened, and I've just got to tell someone.

I know all this may sound very dramatic, but I hope you will understand my excited tone. Many things are not as they were, Pearl, many things.

Perhaps you will think me silly, but, honestly, I've had difficulty in remembering how to spell your name. Isn't it funny how things that can slip one's mind? I used to like seeing forgotten ideas as guests who booked into a hotel expecting all-night parties or a late-bar and found instead they'd been abandoned to themselves. They say forgotten ideas come back to us, but really we return to forgotten ideas. One day something opens the door, Pearl, and we go back in and find the ideas still there, maybe lean and hungry and unshaven by now, but ready and willing to go. Sometimes what you find in an empty room can change your whole life. I know. Nobody knows rooms better than I do.

Do you remember all those years ago in school when we had to write our names repeatedly on the back of long strips of paper? Do you remember that? I don't know what the purpose of it was, but I remember eventually we were so tired we couldn't be sure how to spell our own names any longer. Our own names! So you see, Pearl, it's not such a serious thing, or at least not uncommon, that I forgot. Nothing personal, I assure you. Yes, now I do realize it's not so difficult—H.A.N.D., same as the thing on the end of your arm. But it's easy be clever in retrospect. You do forgive me? I know you forgive me.

Now, I don't really know where to start. How are you? It's been a long time. So much has happened since we last talked—Frank, the kids.... I'm losing myself a bit; it's just that I tend to get giddy when I look back. It's like getting vertigo standing over the past. There's just so much of it!

But I know you must have a lot of questions to ask. There's a lot of blank space to be filled. Where should I start? The kids are all grown up now. Did you know that? Did you imagine them getting older? Richard is almost twelve and Elizabeth is seven. Of course, I don't see them now, but I manage to keep pretty good contact with them. They're really very good. And when you consider how very careful they must be not to be seen!

Elizabeth has agreed a plan with the postman. It's ingenious! When he comes to deliver her father's post, she slips him her notes or snippets of news and he takes them away with him. It's their little secret. Yes, of course, there's a risk involved, but she manages. Often I think what a future she must have, a child with her intelligence. I wonder will she come looking for me when she is old enough to escape. Richard, meanwhile, is like all young boys his age —impulsive, devious, distant. He never puts his mark to any of his sister's letters. But I know he is with her in spirit. And with me. What more could I ask for? When their father brings them into town on Sunday afternoons, she leaves me a message in one of our secret hiding places. Often it is underneath the foot of an equestrian statue just inside the gate, or sometimes it is over on the bandstand, during lunchtime, and I read it sitting in the grass with the brass band playing *Little Brown Jug*. I may think at first it is only a sheet of music one of the musicians has dropped, or a loose page fallen from some student's unbound textbook, but with time I usually manage to recognize her hand or her tone behind the code. As I said, she has to be very careful.

Nothing pleases me more than to find one of Elizabeth's notes on my rounds. They bring warmth and light to my day. And God knows we all need warmth and light. And, of course, I don't like coming home on my own. And the number on the front door hear is just painted on as if a drunk had done it. And it's a damp room.

I'd been here two weeks before I heard anything out of the ordinary. I'd kept busy for the first while collecting furniture and decorations from rubbish skips. Then I found a working wireless and I began to spend more time sitting in and listening to it. Especially the afternoon programmes, the telephone programmes. 'Hello?' And people just tell the whole world how they feel, what they think of such-and-such. It's a fantastic wireless. The programmes that are on it!

The first time it came from under the floor, over by the wash-hand basin. For a while I thought it had something to do with pipes. Then I thought it might be mice. I thought it might be anything except what it was—a voice, Pearl! I was reading my favourite postcard, looking at the picture, imagining a little to the left of the scene, a little to the right, trying to paint in the whole wider picture. And I heard it: the voice.

'Hello.'

It was softer and clearer this time, friendlier—a girl's voice. It was not a noise, Pearl. It was a voice. I went to the bed and examined the wireless. The wireless was off. The plug was pulled out. The voice came from somewhere else in the room. It came from under the floorboards. I ran over to the wash-hand basin and turned the tap on to full. I shifted every board and stick of furniture that I had the strength to shift. I shook the curtains and stamped my heels. 'Out! Out! Out!' The fellow downstairs hit the ceiling with a brush handle or something. He shouted up the stairs, used his filthy words again. So I stopped stamping, turned off the water and decided to go to the park. When I calmed down I realized that I needn't be afraid. After all, what was it only a voice? and I was not afraid of all the new voices on my wireless. So why should I worry about a friendly-sounding one that was coming from behind the wall or underneath the floor over by the wash-hand basin? The voice was a communication. Communication is what has been missing from my life.

Frank frightened me so much sometimes that I would have to escape for a while. When I'd get back we'd exchange apologies for promises and everything would be fine again. For a week or two or three. The last time I got back, he'd gone and taken the kids with him. Where he thought he was going at forty-three and greying I couldn't understand, and I fully expected him back. After all, *I* had always gone back. But he did not come back. And he did not make contact with me. Only Elizabeth has made and continues to make contact with me. This handwritten copy of 'Ode to a Nightingale' is my daughter making contact with me. This postcard from Chile in a foreign language is my daughter making contact with me. This necklace, this pen, these broken sun-glasses, that bag of condoms: this is how she communicates with me.

I came back stronger, thinking of these things, the strength of her love, her faithfulness, growing inside me. I came back to the room and lived with the voice. I listened to it.

In the beginning the voice seemed to sense my unease and would restrict itself to saying hello now and again, and maybe a 'yes' or 'no' here and there. After a time I got to like it in a way. It was reassuring to find it stayed with me, at my pace. I liked to think aloud and the voice would answer, 'Yes, that's a fine idea'. Then one day, all of a sudden, as I was boiling the kettle for tea, the voice said:

'Do you have anything planned for today, _____?' and it called me by my name.

I panicked, I admit. 'What do you know about me?'

'Your name, for a start,' it said, calmly, and it said the word 'name' as if it were trying to provoke me.

Before I knew what I was saying, I'd made a counter-attack.

'And *your* name is Pearl!' I was shocked at my own declaration. It was just something that came to me, on the spur of the moment. I didn't even think about it beforehand.

And I was right! Listen to me: it was your voice, Pearl, your voice in my room talking to me, saying 'hello, yes, no, it's a fine idea'. All that time, it was your voice, and I didn't recognize it.

'I'm surprised it took you so long to recognize me,' said your voice, Pearl. And I apologized. I explained things a bit. Your voice didn't press for details.

Since then things have been different around here. Lots of things have changed, as I've said. Your voice and I, like Elizabeth has done, have established a plan to keep both of us company. When I go out into town I leave the transistor on so that your voice can listen to the telephone programmes or whatever, and report the general picture when I get back. If I miss anything of importance, it will fill me in. If I hear anything of note while I'm in town, or if I find a message from Elizabeth, from the kids, I read it in detail when I get home. We're like those serial detectives, your voice and me, piecing together the clues to get the wider picture — where there are, who they're with, how they are without their mother.

Sometimes your voice and I just go back to old times.
'Little Rosie Bleach?'
No, I think, she never married. Too shy, too quiet.
'And Amanda Clarke?'
Mandy, we agree, probably just stepped from school like an explorer stepping off the edge of the world. How could she have survived in the real world?

And we go right down the whole list of them, Pearl, every single one of them with her hair tied up and her stockings around her ankles. Every one of them, except you. Isn't that funny? We never talk about you.

Anyway, that's about the extent of it. I hope this letter hasn't confused you too much. There is enough confusion in the world without my adding to it. The prospect of your voice underneath my floor or in my walls around the wash-hand basin—it's enough to frighten anyone. But, believe me, the reality of it is much less frightening. I'll write again soon—maybe when I next have more news from the kids. I'll give you an update on the situation. You know I have a photograph of her — Elizabeth. I forgot to tell you, did I? Well, she's beautiful, of course—you'd have guessed that—but so beautiful she stands out from the crowds of children with her. It's a school outing or something, a bad photograph, everyone looks impossibly dark. But even still she shines....

But, Pearl, I've something else to say to you. It's not about the voice. Well, it is about the voice and it's about much more. I've thought about this for a long time now. I've thought it through. Right to the end. I know how it would go, every step of the way and what might happen there. I've been thinking about it, I suppose, since that first night I recognized your voice in my room. It was almost the only thing on my mind as I lay there in the dark in bed. It would be a way for me to have the kids back, have my friends back, all those years that vanished with him. Frank. You could find him, Pearl. You could find the bastard. Tear his heart out.

I have said it now. Tear his heart out. That is enough to say in one letter. That is enough. I've got to go. We have been distant so long it is inevitable that I may seem strange to you as your voice has seemed, until recently, strange to me. Strange but familiar. The lights have gone out in my room, Pearl, it is dark outside, and yet there is a light here to help me finish my letter. I'll tell your voice I wrote to you. I think it thinks this whole situation is very amusing. And perhaps it is right.

Now take care, but bear in mind what I said. It will not be winter always.

Always yours,

Pearl.

FEET ON THE GROUND

Sullivan switched out the light.

'Goodnight,' he said, and answered himself: 'G'night, Bobbie. Sweet dreams.' It was a voice that might have been his father's.

He could hear a cat somewhere and, closer, the whispers of lovers in the shadowed laneway beside the house. His forehead was damp and by now his hands kept sticking to the sheets. He sighed deeply as if to signal to his exhausted body that it was time for sleep.

'Bobbie. Goodnight.'

He remembered the chesty voice, could almost see his father's bearded face in the half-light from the window. Old Billy Sullivan, how he would have had all the young men in the country in bed by ten and up at dawn if he had had his way. That would have toughened them up. Made men of them. None of this unemployment nonsense, none of this hanging around with pub revolutionaries and prophets of doom. What would Old Billy have said if he had been here now to see his son, his grown son, like this? Did he ever seriously consider what the future might hold for his family, his community? Did he think that what he saw beginning in fits and starts around him might continue for all these years and claim all these lives on both sides?

Bobbie remembered evenings when his father, in a string vest, would sit and read travel books in his bedroom, books about ships, foreign lands, active volcanoes. He remembered how his return from the bedroom and all this exotica inevitably left him in a low mood, and how he would stand by the window watching the city lean towards war outside. Once in a while his mother would send Bobbie up to bed before his father had emerged, and Bobbie would undress and lie quietly in bed waiting for his father's last words of the evening, 'G'night, Bobbie'—a voice that would fall away before the darkness.

He sat up in bed and switched on the light. What was happening to him? Why had that voice returned from his childhood?

The room around him was as it had been minutes before, covered with scattered pieces of clothing, smelling of cigarette ends, spilt beer. He pulled back the covers and swung his legs round so that he sat upright with his feet on the ground. For a second he almost smiled. Everything was silent again. His father had left him.

It had always made Sullivan smile to find his feet on the ground. How he had once envied his father and the older boys in church, the way they could sit with their feet firmly settled, while *his* swung embarrassingly above the kneeler. Younger boys than he could be seen to bridge the gap with their longer legs—something he'd have traded his oldest comic for, though he never spoke of it to anyone. For years he assumed everyone had a personal crisis of the sort. For years he just seemed to swing, to reach nothing. And his father, mercifully, seemed not to notice.

Now, of course, he could only remember a fraction of the feelings that he had had back then. He was clearly no longer a boy, and there was no one left to remark on the way his feet touched ground, or on the black bristles on his chin which he would have borne with pride as a teenager. There was no one now to admire the dark stab of hair on his belly just above his belt buckle. No one: a few voices, a ghost or two, no one who would take any notice of a 30-year old schoolboy.

Outside it was beginning to drizzle. A car drove slowly by. Sullivan listened without enthusiasm. He switched out the light and moved to the window to watch it pass. Exhaustion had removed almost all fear from his mind.

The car turned the corner at the top of the street. It was difficult to say how many passengers there had been, or whether they had been wearing uniforms. There had been no time for a clear look. Anyway, he reflected, uniforms were no threat to him. He had had his encounter with uniforms, and survived. They would not come bursting into his room in the middle of the night again, waving their guns and flashlights, shouting in their foreign accents.... He was a free man and would stay so.

Sullivan was not one to scare easily. That was why it had been him out there that night. They had known they could depend on him, knew that he wouldn't prove to be just talk and drink when it came to the crunch. They had had faith in him. They had trusted him to perform efficiently, and he had not disappointed them. He would continue to live up to their expectations. Their faith had not been misplaced. Their relationship was a religious thing....

Something crackled up at the end of the street—a voice, one of those ghostly voices that only appear in troubled places, electronic voices, voices of machines that haunt the streets.

'Foxtrot, Bravo, Foxtrot...' Sullivan listened dreamily. He'd grown up within earshot of those voices, had even called himself Charlie Delta at school, a favourite name for his detective adventures in the derelict houses.

Charles. It had also been the name of the man that night. Not so much coincidence as inevitability. With a past as gross and ever-expanding as his own, one was bound to feel the pull of its gravity from time to time. What might this Charles have been like? Maybe his wife had called him Charlie, too—a name that once meant to Sullivan only happy childhood days spent searching for any old thing to hide in his biscuit-tin in the jungle that passed for their back garden.

How that October night had changed his past—even his childhood—as well as determining his future.

'Times change,' he said aloud, repeating his mother's weary and well-worn observation, and then, surprised at the sound of his own voice in the darkness, he exhaled heavily and sat back on the bed.

What was it others had done in this situation? He was, after all, certainly not the first. There had been two others that month, he remembered—as if that October were something he would ever forget! How did those others sleep now, all this time later, wherever they were, scattered around the city, in prisons north or south, or living new lives without pasts in Boston or Chicago.

What was it like to never talk of it to anyone? to be a child always with some terrible secret in the garden?

After four and a half years, he felt he was no closer to the answer.

A helicopter trimmed the warm hush of night-time over the identical houses.

Sullivan's mind returned to drink, a favourite thought. Maybe there, after all, he could lose himself. Nobody cared what some drunk said. Most of the crowd in his local had 'confessed' to an apocalypse or two in their time, and there had been enough statues blown apart by the bar's clientele to suggest that the island had once been populated by creatures of stone. Down there they would view his activities as admirable, enviable. They would buy him a drink and lose interest when he refused to exaggerate.

'In the head? Oh, fair play. That must have been something.' The old fellow with the crutch might even spit in his palm for a handshake, the one who had known his father.

But eventually they would return to their silences, their newspapers, their dreams, their grim realities. None of them would be coming back with Sullivan to his room to see what was waiting there. None of them would spend a sleepless night hearing, over and over, but somewhere out of reach, the startled shout, the chair thrown back, the gunshots echoing up the street. Or see that young girl standing in her hallway, still holding a front door which, for the rest of her life, she would open and reopen guiltily in her nightmares.

Without knowing anything else about this child—this young woman by now!—Sullivan knew their night-

mares on different sides of the city began that same
October night.

No. He could not bear the patronizing talk of the pub,
the faked empathies. He would remain where he was,
perhaps even stay out of work for a day or two, until this
unease might pass. What was his name who'd fixed him
up when he'd had that accident with the cables...? *He'd*
cover for him. Not the worst, for one of them. Sullivan
recalled the surprise of his work-mates when he'd turned
up before the end of that week, his arm in a sling and a
brace on his neck.

'I was bored,' he'd joked, making screwdriver motions
with a finger to his broken arm. He had enjoyed being
the hard man. It felt good to be taken seriously.

He remembered the day when as a child his biscuit-
tin had been discovered.

'Bobbie, do you know what this is?' His father had
feared the answer. It was not the first time his seven-
year-old son had seen a live round.

'Do you know how dangerous this is?'

'I know,' was all the young Bobbie had said in his
defence.

But why was he remembering this? What had biscuit-
tins got to do with anything?

He climbed back into bed and pulled a crumpled sheet
across himself. Almost immediately, he saw the little girl
in the doorway, her father over the chair, his backside
still in the seat, one foot suspended, lifeless in the air.

'Bobbie,' said his father's voice, darkly. Sullivan
struggled to recall the face, the thin features... But all that
came to him were impressions, a vague inheritance—
long nose, dimple, that deep voice.... Nothing else had

survived those years, that house. Not a photograph, not a page of one of his father's precious journals.

That day he'd stood before the charred ruins of the house, all he had been able to think of was Charlie Delta searching for clues, ferreting for bits of brass or love letters to take home to his secret trove—Charlie Delta striding down the street in his false nose, black moustache and spectacles... But tonight he had nowhere left to go home to.

'Bobbie.'

It was hard now to see anything against the light of that remembered doorway held open to the city in evening time. It was hard for Sullivan to see anything but a young girl silhouetted, a jumble of telephone books behind her in a hallway.

And there was nothing to be heard except the ticking of his wrist-watch on the sideboard, the imaginary sweep of a foot that would never reach the ground.

BEFORE JULIA GETS HOME

Sidney Brolly had had enough of doctors, psychiatrists and seventh sons. There was only exorcism left down that road. This time he would treat her with humour.

Smithfield market at six in the morning was a side of Dublin Sidney had never seen or, if he had, one he had long forgotten. He was shocked at how *real* it all was— the fruit traders loading and unloading, the van drivers with their hands deep in their pockets, and a gang of somewhat threatening horse-merchants exhibiting their T-shirts and kick-scars with pride. Sidney could feel goose-flesh on his arms..

But best of all were the horses, and, before he knew quite what he was doing he had chosen a big, friendly-looking one just minutes after its arrival, self-consciously paid cash on the spot, and found a young man who agreed to ride it home for him in exchange for a pack of cigarettes and the bus fare back to town.

The horse was brown—to go with the carpets.

True, there were a couple of moments when he wondered if he were doing the right thing. But the challenge of having to conceal the beast before Julia might get home was more than Sidney could resist. And, after all, difficult situations called for difficult measures.

It would be the perfect surprise.

And so he managed to survive, for instance, the half hour he spent watching Danno strolling brazenly about the house until the morning buses would begin. Sidney kept himself occupied in pretending to dust down the book-shelves and the dressing table with his passport and his wife's jewellery inside. And when Danno had finally gone, and with the cigarette smoke still clearing through the opened windows, Sidney went back through the house nervously making an inventory of chairs and tables.

When at last he had checked and double-checked his findings, he felt sure that his anxiety was merely the upset of having a stranger in their home. He allowed himself sit back in Julia's rocking chair and plan the concealing of the horse. But, unaccustomed to such early mornings, and tired from his adventures, it was not long before he had drifted off into a light snooze.

He came to with the sensation that something was not quite right. For a moment he sat with his head quizzically tipped to one side. Then the sight of a large, malodorous deposit at his feet reminded him that he had a guest. And, after all, if the animal were to be a surprise as intended— a sign that, however terrible things might seem, he had not forgotten how to charm her—it was of absolute importance that it be well concealed before Julia's return.

However, as it transpired, this did not prove a simple matter.

The first and most obvious place to try was the spare room downstairs. As luck would have it, something about the room—perhaps the dust, or the smell of the mothballs hanging behind the curtains—began to irritate the horse to such a degree that it was the most Sidney could do just to get him out of there without putting a hoof through the thin wall.

Come on, you old fool, he told himself, you knew this wasn't going to be easy.

And so with his left hand pegging his nostrils, he scooped up the newly-discovered pile of droppings from the floor and flipped them thoughtfully out the back window and into her rose bed.

Fortunately the house was still in one piece. The horse stood motionless and co-operative, if a little surprised to find himself in the living room of Sidney's small, tidy home.

Sidney smiled at the idea. He even allowed himself a giggle. But where was he going to conceal the thing?

The problem was not altogether unfamiliar, not in style at least. There had, alas, been times beyond recall when he'd asked himself questions which had ended with '...before Julia gets home?' Everything had to be hidden away before that dangerous hour—knives, razors, poisons, pills—even the Black & Decker, when it had been working. In fact, all his toys. On more than one occasion he had just snapped shut the lock on the tool-shed door and had turned around to find that she had crept up on him from behind. And, though taking away her house keys had removed at least one part of that fear, the problem today was considerably bigger than anything before. At a push he might once have managed to slip a carving knife down his pants and pass her sideways but amicably in the hallway: 'Ah, you're home, dear.' He might even have managed to place a kiss on her cheek in passing. But clearly he could not stick a horse down his pants.

He would think about it some more.

It was already dark when Sidney finally fell over in a deep sleep onto the settee, leaving the horse now known as Trigger, himself sleeping, stood with his face against the cold of the window pane. At least this was how Sidney found him when he was awoken just before nine on the following morning by a persistent ringing at the door.

'Oh my God!' He searched for his watch. Julia was home, and there was a horse in her kitchen!

Suddenly the idea had lost all its charm. What would she say? He could imagine her shrieking uncontrollably or crying, stooped on her brittle legs to pick up the remains of the vase, broken the previous evening, or the pieces of her therapeutic jigsaws. Sidney was consumed by confusion. He must hide the horse. But where? Was that not the problem which had defeated him last night and forced him to seek refuge in sleep?

He scanned the room frantically. Whatever had gotten into him!

Then it came to him.

'Ah, Mr Brolly?'

He opened the door to find a man standing there, his face and arms covered in black dust.

Sidney stared.

'Coal delivery,' said the man, pointing to the bag at his feet.

Sidney hadn't noticed it at first; now he stared at it.

'Not Julia,' he calmed himself.

The man seemed puzzled. He lifted the bag.

'In here?'

It was already too late to stop him.

'The hallway is fine,' Sidney said, ineffectually.

He stood on the doorstep, looking down the hill. What he was looking for he didn't know, but he counted to ten and then to ten again, and even held his breath. When he looked around, the coalman was standing behind him staring back at the very large object draped with table cloth and curtains.

'Eh, what is it?' he said, half turning.

'A surprise,' was all Sidney could think to say.

Putting porridge on the cooker for Trigger and some toast on for himself, Sidney felt his old doubts begin to resurface, and he found himself resigned once again to the horse's removal. What kind of crazy scheme had been in his head? Perhaps Julia had been right and he was watching too much of that new television. Perhaps it did make people do peculiar things after all.

As he was pondering this, and trying to come to some conclusion as to what to do, the doorbell rang for the second time.

As quietly as he could, he crept around to the downstairs bathroom to peep out. The next train which might be carrying Julia was not due until noon. He would have to be careful about opening the door to anyone else lest the secret get out and the men in white coats come to take *him* away.

Miraculously, Trigger remained quiet in the kitchen.

When he pulled back the lace curtain, Sidney saw Fr Mahoney standing there.

'Oh dear...'

Fr Mahoney stepped back from the door, adjusted his spectacles and frowned at each and every window on the house in turn. He was the type of priest who was always frowning, especially at people like Sidney who had drifted away from the church. Long and hard he stared at the house as if he knew Sidney, the lost sheep, were inside, almost within reach.

Sidney watched in silence, breathlessly.

Just then Trigger sneezed.

'Brolly?' The priest sprang forward, his fingers in the letterbox. 'Brolly, are you in there?'

Sidney could feel tears well up in his eyes. Now the church had become involved!

The priest stood back and paused. He seemed unsure about something. As if on second thought, he turned and walked slowly down the garden towards the road.

Suddenly he stopped. Sidney was almost afraid to look. He could see Fr Mahoney absolutely motionless by the yellow wooden gate. Standing on his tip-toes by the high window-sill, he followed the long dark figure reluctantly to its feet.

The priest had stood in one of Trigger's 'gifts'!

Prayer was the first thing that came to Sidney Brolly's mind, but he thought it best to keep out of God's way for the time being.

'Brolly!' the priest was calling for the whole neighbourhood to hear, breaking the name into three syllables as he jerked his foot up and back in the freshly-mown grass. But even now Sidney thought he detected a note of uncertainty in the priest's voice. Perhaps if he could stay perfectly quiet and if Trigger could be kept away from the window....

'Brolly, what's going on in there?' Fr Mahoney was back, this time banging with his fist on the door.

'Are you all right in there? Look, this is no time for games.'

Sidney crouched before the horse and shook from head to toe.

He crouched there in terror until the knocking and shouting had stopped. He listened and heard nothing, but he knew it would be dangerous to assume that this was any guarantee that the priest had gone. Perhaps he had merely removed his shoes to clean them and was, at that very moment, creeping around outside, peering through the windows, memorizing every detail for Sidney's next visit to the confession box. Oh the horror of that little room.... Sidney wondered how any God could resort to such humiliations.

He caught hold of himself. He turned to Trigger. The horse had now taken to pulling straw from the back of Julia's rocking chair. The whole affair was getting impossibly out of hand.

'Dok dok,' said Sidney, urgently, trying to imitate the sound that other people made when they fancied they could communicate with horses. Trigger, of course, ignored him.

'Dok, dok, dok...'

And then it started.

First it came quietly. Not even Trigger, now right beside him, noticed anything. What would Fr Mahoney say to him when the truth came out? Sidney tried to imagine the admonishments, tried to sober himself, but instead all he could think of was the priest in stocking feet, tip-toeing about the garden.

There was nothing else for it. He stood up helplessly and pushed past the horse, elbowing him good-humouredly on the rump.

And Julia due home any minute....

He could no longer contain himself. He waddled into the hall, laughing now so much he could hardly see. Trigger whinnied loudly in the background which only made the situation more fantastic.

Embracing the inevitable, he opened the door.

'I give up,' he said, hands above his head, tears streaming from his eyes.

But Fr Mahoney was gone.

It was now 10.15 and the next train was due at 12.00. Julia would be on it.

But somehow encouraged by his change of humour since the priest's call, Sidney had once again set about the task of concealing Trigger for the purpose of a surprise. In the twenty-four hours of their relationship, his life had already taken a turn much for the better. Gone was the routine of suburban house husbandry, gone the monotony of his days alone, his days waiting for them to send her back. Once again he felt the refreshing breeze of risk. He attributed this, naturally, to the horse's presence. Already he could feel something of a relationship developing. Indeed, there seemed an air of enterprise in 'Mountain View' which he had not experienced since his retirement. Soon, he knew, he would pass his elation on to Julia.

With renewed enthusiasm he set about the task. Returning from the tool shed he found Trigger completely accustomed to his surroundings, chewing away on Julia's rocking chair as if it had been left there solely for that purpose. For Sidney it seemed a small price to pay for peace and quiet. He would throw a blanket over the holes and have them repaired the next time Julia was away.

The hammering and sawing lasted no more than half an hour. Sidney's creation covered the whole of the floor before him, and there was sawdust over his clothes and even in his hair. For a moment Trigger seemed to inspect the work but then resumed his meal.

Within the hour, Sidney was sitting down for tea and a well-deserved scone, his hair combed and his best mustard jumper on. The only indication of the work that had been done was a small sticking plaster on his thumb where he had taken a splinter.

'Tap once for yes, twice for no,' he whispered in his best horror-film voice, and he laughed so hard that the tea spilled down his freshly-laundered pants, and he had to change for the second time in as many minutes.

Somewhere behind the new partition, Trigger seemed to sigh.

Just as he was coming down the stairs from the bedroom, all fresh and new again, he heard her taxi draw up outside. He smiled.

'Now, Trigger, you just stay perfectly still until I give the word, understand? Not a whisper.'

He walked to the door, pausing a moment before the mirror to flatten down his fringe and straighten the tie ridge under his jumper. His face looked tired and flushed, older than its fifty-seven years.

Suddenly something blue flashed across his face: a light. It flashed again.

Against the frosted glass he could just about make out the shadows of three or four people with the blue light flashing behind them. He could hear Fr Mahoney's voice.

For a moment Sidney thought he would faint. Someone had called the Police!

'Trigger, what shall I do?' He was back in the kitchen, giggling and shaking with fear, whispering to the newly-erected wall. It felt like being in church and remembering a favourite joke. But he doubted if the Police would find it funny.

'Mr Brolly?'—a familiar voice was calling his name.

'Please open up, Mr Brolly.'

Sidney recognized it.

'I'm here, Father,' he croaked, coming to the door. There seemed no point in postponing the inevitable. They knew. Everyone knew. His madness would soon be known to the world.

The policemen jumped back when he opened the door; one of them even removed his cap in confusion.

'Mr Brolly!' said a stranger.

Sidney ignored him. All of 'Mountain Road' were out, folded arms everywhere, the blue light on the Police car calling others out to witness his stupidity. Any moment now her taxi would pull up....

Fr Mahoney spoke gravely.

'Mr Brolly... Sidney...'

Sidney, too, was looking for words.

'Father, I know you'll find this hard to believe...'

Suddenly the policemen sidled past him and into the house.

'There's something burning in here!'

The second policeman followed.

'Eh, that will be the porridge,' Sidney called after them, smiling like a lunatic at the priest. 'You see, Father...'

Suddenly there was a splintering sound from inside followed by a loud whinnying and a crash of glass.

Sidney smiled weakly.

'Mr Brolly,' said the man in the dark suit, and he stopped short again, leaving Sidney to wonder where he had seen that face before.

Silently the policemen came out, dusting themselves down and staring incredulously at each other.

'I'm sorry,' continued Fr Mahoney, extending a bony hand, 'I'm afraid it's Julia.'

A Question of Innocence

Madigan prayed that the telephone would ring, but that there would be no one on the line. He seldom prayed but, like all atheists, when he did he did not take it lightly. That prayers were sitting on his lips at all, and had survived within him somewhere since childhood, must have been a sign of something. Or so many would have told him. But did he believe that? Or was it not simply a case of convenience? Would he not as readily have given himself to the occult, to Abracadabra or bubble, bubble, what was it? toil and trouble, if that had been part of his childhood experience? He consoled his disbelieving heart, played these usual games with himself and prayed it would ring. It would be easier to talk to a fictitious caller than to sit here with Burke, Burke who simply stared ahead of him into space.

How was Madigan to have known such a simple question would cause this terrible change in his partner's humour? He scolded himself for accepting the older man's invitation to stay on for a drink after their secretaries had packed up and gone for the weekend. He had spent a year and a half avoiding such intimacies.

Why had he given in to today's invitation? He knew he should have trusted his instincts.

He also knew he could sit there until kingdom come, and still Burke would not unburden himself of whatever was troubling him. He stared at the older man with something approaching disgust, a disgust he felt, outside of his control, for all sick things.

So he waited, sipped his drink, and found himself drawn back to what was the most remarkable house in his own memory. Even now the image of the place was enough to send a shiver down his spine.

The house in which he found himself was like a museum whose exhibits had been not so much arranged as abandoned wherever they might fit. Not that it had been an unattractive arrangement: *au contraire*, as its owner had been fond of saying. Its fascination lay in the very fact that it was so haphazard, so surprising. It was a different wonderland for everyone who visited, and sometimes even seemed to change identity from one visit to the next, depending on which wing, which door, one entered through. The sequence of rooms visited, the light or lack of it penetrating the oak trees all around, the time of day, the season—all revealed new aspects of the labyrinth, suggested new chronologies for the vast collection of art and artefact. Madigan recalled Nobel's delight in taking visitors through the rooms and corridors and attempting to confuse their opinions on what had been influenced by what. His idea had been that all art and design exists simultaneously, and the arbitrary sequence of its discovery points only to our restricting concepts of time. He had been confident that he would one day win the prize of his namesake in acknowledgement of his contribution to the way we think about the world.

In other words he had been a 'headcase', cut off from reality in the great Gormenghast of his possessions. Madigan smiled at the raw word he had not used in years, but immediately shuddered when he recalled his first visit to the house, and the numerous times he had gone back on his own in the late afternoons of that last summer of innocence. Hungry for education outside of school, and fascinated by the French stranger who allowed him to smoke cigarettes freely and often gave him a glass of wine when there was something 'worthy' in the cellar, he could not avoid the house, its claustrophobic vastness.

Hearing a noise from Burke, he abandoned his daydream. The senior partner of Burke, Madigan & Co., Auctioneers was now actually holding the gin bottle. Progress at last! Madigan extended his glass for a refill. Perhaps a half hour of quiet recollection was not such a bad thing....

But Burke was making no move to pour. Instead he seemed to be checking that the bottle was still there, that he was still there by inference.

Madigan slumped back in his chair. How long would this go on? How long would Burke continue to avoid his eyes, unprepared for conversation without the protecting light of alcohol to guide him? He felt himself grow impatient and knew it would not be long before his impatience turned to anger. Say something, you silly old bastard! Burke said nothing.

Madigan stood and walked over to the full-length window which looked down on the high street. The Friday evening traffic, the throngs of pedestrians.... Out there was the city and, beyond it, way beyond it, Nobel's house, empty, its floorboards rotted.

Why was he thinking like this? Behind him sat Burke, a forgotten cigarette quenched by a tear between his stubby, browned fingers. He had been on the point of shouting when he had noticed the older man's tears.

Maybe I could tell him about the house, about Nobel? Maybe I could have done with it. When he hears what I have to say, maybe he won't feel so bad. He may even want to open up....

But the excitement soon deserted him and he sat down and lit himself a cigarette.

'Tell me, Harry.' He felt more than a little awkward about the implied intimacy of using Burke's Christian name.

Burke looked up. There was a moment after his eyes had settled on Madigan's moustache when it seemed as if the effort of turning his head would twist his whole body out of the chair and onto the floor. Madigan wondered if his tone had been too harsh. He wished Burke would look him in the eye for once, just once.

He again held out his empty glass. When Burke finally began to pour, he spilled most of the remainder over his pants.

Maybe that was what Burke had had in mind all along, thought Madigan. Maybe staying on in the office to get drunk and have a good cry was his idea of release. I have better things to do with my time than to sit here playing nurse to old idiots like him! Pour the drink, for Jesus' sake!

He screwed his cigarette into the ashtray and forced his shoulders and arms to relax. Why did Burke annoy him so? Why did he feel so wound up, so close to fury?

An ornament on the mantelpiece caught his attention. Netsuke—a Japanese belt button. He had often wondered if it had been their respective loves of rare things that had brought them together. The netsuke on the mantelpiece more than anything. Hadn't they spent as much of the original meeting talking about it as they had about his academic qualifications?

But the ornament brought him back further still to the place where he had learned an appreciation of such exotic things. Nobel's collection of things Japanese had been just another marvel in a house of seemingly countless fascinations. But, with what he had since learned about antiques, he was now able to identify many of the artists whose work his boyhood enthusiasm had preserved with an almost photographic memory. How much of it he had seen for sale in showrooms since he had joined Burke's practice just eighteen months before.... Even now, so much later, it was almost frightening to look on it again as if, around the most beautiful of the *objets d'art,* the gloom of the old house— all old houses—still clung on like a shadow.

He recalled distinctly his last trip to the house, remembered climbing the grand staircase with the paintings down either side, strolling down the dark corridors, tripping over things, already a stolen cigarette lighting in his mouth.

'Mr Nobel, it's Philip—Philippe!'

Did he imagine it, or had Burke noticed the panic which this memory brought on? Madigan saw there were again tears, and again he felt ashamed of his inability to communicate with the older man. He wondered if it would have been different had Burke been a woman? Would they have been able to show each other more compassion?

The idea of going over to Burke, of gently removing the empty bottle from his grasp, of embracing him warmly, did occur to him. But he dismissed it. It was not that he was afraid that such a gesture might be misunderstood—there could be nothing more natural than to embrace a troubled colleague. It was simply that to touch another human being in this way, let alone an older man perfumed by cigarettes and alcohol, was to walk again that corridor in his school pants and tie, completely unaware of what was about to happen. There was nothing he could do. Just to sit there alone with Burke was, in a way, to brave again those endless expanses of shadow between windows, to scarcely have exploited the few bands of sunlight before he was again in darkness.

He checked his watch. For almost all of two hours they had sat there without conversation. The shops would have closed by now and there was nothing to eat in his flat. He did not relish the prospect of another cheap restaurant on his own.

'Harry, look, are you all right?'

Burke lowered his head and sobbed.

In his wildest dreams, Madigan could never have pictured this. The sight both frightened and, he had to confess, reassured him. He wondered again at the repercussions of his innocent question which seemed to have reduced two grown men to frightened children. Even with the success of their practice—a busy office on the high street, two secretaries, a list of impressive, international clients—they had never become any closer than that initial handshake which had sealed the partnership.

His disgust for Burke had now come back on himself. What, after all, had *he* done to build a friendship? What, if anything, had he told anyone about himself? That his flat was always in a mess and he couldn't care or cook for himself? That his fear of big country houses had never gone away? That the feeling of horror, of disgrace never, never goes away?

'Jesus, Mr Burke, this is ridiculous!' His patience finally left him. He pushed back the swivel chair and grabbed his coat.

'Helen,' Burke whispered. 'She's left me.'

Madigan felt something loosen in his stomach at the sound of a woman's name. His breath left him. (He was more drunk than he had supposed.) In front of Burke he noticed, not for the first time, but for the first time tonight, a photograph of a grey-haired middle-aged woman in a cardigan and jeans. Was he really so slow? How had he failed to understand before now?

The room heaved as Madigan moved towards Burke, putting his hand as softly as he could on the crouched man's shoulder. The face in the photograph watched him with a saint's eyes as he struggled to disregard the remembered smells of polished floors and French cigarettes.

THE MAN WHO ATE STONES

Sammy was watching eggs fry when he heard a familiar sound outside, as if a mountain were being dragged over the restaurant floor.

'C-Cigarette, Mr Holland?' he stuttered, emerging from the steamy kitchen.

'You know what I want.' Holland looked the slight waiter in the eye. 'And it isn't on the menu either.'

Already he'd got his feet up on a table and was swinging his knuckles over the worn carpet to either side of his chair legs. He was obviously enjoying this.

Sammy was trying to think of a way to break the news gently to Fahy. It was not something he suspected the cook would want to hear.

'OK,' he said to Holland in a half-pitying, half you-asked-for-it tone—the real house speciality in his uncle's unpopular restaurant.

Nothing had gone right in the Bamboo Grove all day; there had been numerous complaints about the food, and now here was Holland yet again, as if life wasn't impossible enough already. Sammy could hardly wait for closing time. He wished he could leave right now, walk right out the door and leave Holland and Fahy to sort things out between themselves.

He had dreamt of refusing Holland before—not because he had anything against the fellow or his peculiar tastes; in a restaurant you soon got used to those. No, the real problem was not so much Holland, as having to face the ever-complaining cook as though Holland's order were some form of personal vendetta which Sammy himself had cooked up. So to speak. To be honest, Sammy had long suspected that much of the hatred between himself and Fahy had its origins in the age-old rivalry between their extreme body types. (Hadn't he even had dreams of Conan-style battles between them, epics he alone attended in the cinema of his bed or behind the microwave? Sammy V The Endomorph!)

Much of the time, however, the cook's enmity manifested itself in anti-Chinese jokes, and no amount of protesting on Sammy's part could make any difference.

'Irish? About as Irish as Egg Fried Rice.'

Holland, meanwhile, was waiting, and Fahy was, as always, in the kitchen frying inexplicably large quantities of eggs for the non-existent customers.

12.45. Not long to go now, thought Sammy. Soon all of it would be behind him. He sneaked a glimpse at the photograph of Alice in his pocket, felt Holland's impatient glare on the back of his neck, and made up his mind. Having listened carefully at the 'out' door, and having heard nothing he went through.

A fan in the corner succeeded in merely stirring up further the oppressive smells of cabbages, meat and eggs. He remembered an old Indian telling him of his first visit to the 'so-called civilized West'—how the smell of meat hung on the breath of the locals, and in their homes, and how it lingered after them even in their places of worship. Sammy himself had almost fainted once passing through the aura of a slaughterhouse concealed behind shop façades. He was so disgusted by the experience that he had vowed to abstain from meat thereafter. Why should he take part in the customs of this land which was not really his? It did not matter that he had been born and raised here. After all, the truth was that he had always been an outsider, a cuckoo raised by a carnivorous foster mother—the West.

'What is it?' boomed Fahy, seeing the waiter standing there. The eggs sizzled like aliens on a transporter pad. Sammy almost laughed aloud.

'Why do you always come in through the 'out' door, you fool? Are you stupid?' The cook glared at him.

Sammy looked around for a moment at the steam-yellowed walls, wondering how his uncle could ever have let the place fall into such disrepair. (Actually he was savouring the moment, the suspense, the potency of bad news.)

He spoke the name as softly as he could: 'Holland.'

'No!' A ladle thrown against the fan made him duck for protection.

'I won't do it. Get him out. It's you!' Fahy was pointing menacingly at him. '*You* encourage people like him with your foreign ideas!'

Sammy was tempted to laugh. People like *him?*

'Right,' said the cook. Sammy looked up in surprise. Trembling with anger, Fahy jerked opened the back door and rummaged for a moment outside.

'Here, give him that and tell him to clear off.' He rattled a large plateful of gravel with a few larger stones in the centre. Pebbles showered down on the metallic work-top he slid it across so abruptly. Sammy took the plate and left the cook kicking wildly at the back door which refused now to close.

Just before the swinging 'out' door, Sammy paused to arrange the larger stones in a pattern, keeping the long ones together on one side so that the plate looked like a meal whose ingredients could be distinguished, if not by taste, then at least by shape. He had often thought how remarkable it was that a human being could become accustomed to almost anything. Here he was, a fairly sane person, of average size and appetites, with a healthy mistrust of religion, politics and take-away foods, of average education—not carrying a percussion instrument for a head, as was the case with Fahy there—and what was this, only the third or fourth time Holland had come in and ordered stones, and already he accepted the whole thing as perfectly normal, thinking now more about how he should present it than wondering at the absurdity of it all. He couldn't even remember at what point the sight of Holland scooping gravel into his mouth had ceased to be a cause of amazement or horror. In fact, he couldn't say for certain if it ever had been! Being constantly surrounded by the meat, blood and stench of the kitchen, he wondered if he didn't secretly welcome the huge earth-eater, the geophagist, who at least caused no fuss about under-cooking or over-cooking or being poisoned. In fact the only thing that weighed against the practice was the noise, the terrible scraping—and the occasional plate shattered by a dropped morsel.

'About time,' said Holland, looking up to find the waiter in a trance beside him.

'And what's this?'

Sammy was silent. 'This' was obviously a plateful of stones.

'Shale, scree, shingle, gravel, pebbles—sedimentary, volcanic...? What is it?'

'Local council, I think,' said Sammy. He left the plate down on the table. 'They're digging outside.' He backed away to a comfortable distance.

'Dumb waiter,' grinned Holland.

Most people would have described Holland as a well-built man, *built* being the operative word. Nobody knew what he did for a living but, on reflection, Sammy supposed one did not need to do anything to be able to afford to dine on stone. Nevertheless, Holland was always well-dressed and, if he could resist the temptation to pick up a piece of the planet and eat it, he would not have appeared out-of-place in the average crowd.

Sammy watched him now as he stared without apparent emotion at the plate. Certainly the big man with the dry grey hair and wide shoulders didn't seem to enjoy his food. But that came as no real surprise. And when he'd stand to leave he would look decidedly uncomfortable. And then he might not be seen for days. Perhaps he was off having his stomach excavated by amateur archaeologists.... Sammy wondered if he didn't secretly eat at one of the other Chinese restaurants the rest of the time, one that served proper Chinese food—not bloody fries and chips—and was run by people like himself who dreamed of some day returning home, encouraged by the recent swing towards private enterprise.

But the difference between Sammy and the others was that Sammy *would* return. He would leave Holland here eating his stones, leave Fahy up to his neck in kitchen slime.... They had talked about it. Alice had agreed. She had agreed. She would call tonight when the restaurant was closed and they would take the money his uncle had left him and go. He would abandon Holland like the rest of them, one of the stone gods of Easter Island.

Alice! He had almost forgotten about her. She would call soon to make arrangements. Sammy could feel his heart beat faster.

Holland ate with no condiments, raking the gravel with his fork. He seemed cautious if not downright suspicious about something. Perhaps it was that he was allergic to granite or something, Sammy laughed to himself. Then he noticed the huge man staring directly into his face. He began to inch back little by little, trying to discover the invisible boundary outside of which he would be permitted to stand and watch. Tonight his curiosity had finally gotten the better of him. Perhaps because it was his last.

He had now backed right up to the swinging door and could hear Fahy mumbling and rattling about inside. He wished for once he could go in there and give the cook a piece of his mind. He was, after all, in a manner, the most important member of staff, being related to the boss. There could be no restaurant without his patience, his waiting—in every sense of the word. Had he no right to assert his authority? But the mere notion of an encounter with the cook chilled him to the bone. It would be so much easier to run away with Alice without a word to any of them. That would be adequate revenge for their years of persecuting him.

Holland had raised the first spoonful of stones to his lips and was holding it there.

Time to exit, thought Sammy, pushing back through the 'out' door and hitting Fahy squarely in the face.

'Christ!' said Fahy, tottering backwards but showing no signs of pain. 'Is he eating it?'

It was a remarkably stupid question, one which could not go unremarked.

'I don't know,' said Sammy. 'He's out there and I'm in here.' It was the first time he had held his ground with the cook. And it felt good.

Fahy returned to his grill and pans while he searched his repertoire of grunts for a suitable reply.

Sammy returned to the restaurant, somewhat heartened. But in moments his mood had turned to one of anxious waiting as he sat by the telephone. 12.45. It wasn't like Alice to be late.

12.45!

'Oh hell; it's stopped!' He jumped to his feet. His first instinct was to run into the kitchen where he found Fahy grinning. Sammy reasoned with himself that the cook was grinning only because that's what morons do when they're cooking eggs for non-existent customers. He was sure Fahy had no idea of his plans. He wondered if it might not have been Holland who was up to no good, but something told him that a man who ate stones would not have been bothered to tamper with restaurant clocks. A man who ate stones was more likely to measure time in thousands of years, to understand no period shorter than the interim between megalithic and neolithic. Yet, if the cook had been the culprit, Sammy could not bring himself to an accusation.

He dashed back out to the window and pulled back the curtain. It was still dark. Time had been reduced to a binary system in which he had to attempt to locate himself with accuracy. All he knew was that it was night, and he felt something of what it must have been like for Holland, to be at the mercy of those slow erosions.

Did this mean the end of all his plans with Alice? Had she given up on him? He found himself pacing about the restaurant.

'You've got a problem,' drawled Holland, who was trying to finish his plateful of stone. It wasn't easy to understand why he kept returning. Sammy was surprised at the conversational tone in Holland's voice.

'Look at me,' he said, holding out his arms like a dancer. 'Chinese and never been to China!' He had decided to get in at the deep end.

Holland put a sharp white stone in his mouth, knocked it around and swallowed with difficulty.

'Guess where I've never been?' he said, and seemed to crack a smile.

The telephone rang.

'Alice!' Sammy sprinted for the kitchen, leaving Holland to gaze wistfully out at the night.

'Alice? Where have you been?'

Fahy came through, putting on his coat, listening with his normally imperceptible chin jutting out. Time for home. He was taking care to conceal the heart and kidneys he had slipped into his bag.

'...But I've got the money organized and everything....'

Fahy picked his nose and flicked the offending article away. He stood in the doorway, watching Sammy for a moment, and then he left without a word.

'Alice...?' The line went dead.

Holland was still seated in the restaurant, eating the last of his stones, when Sammy drew up a chair and sat beside him.

'She's not coming. She thought it was a joke.'

'An Alice who doesn't want to go to Wonderland,' mused Holland.

Sammy looked at the empty plate.

'You want one on the house?' He could not let Holland leave now.

'Sure. Looks like neither of us has anything better to do.'

Sammy stood up and turned towards the kitchen.

'Eh,' said Holland, 'look, do you mind if I come along? Maybe choose my own this time? It's not something everybody would know about, bu your cook here is a bit heavy on the limestone.'

Sammy couldn't be sure if this was a joke or not, but he decided to risk a snigger. Holland did not seem unduly upset.

'Have you ever thought of stones?' he said as they passed through the 'out' door into the kitchen.

Already the grease around the eggs was beginning to harden and turn white.

'Not before tonight,' said Sammy, tugging at the stubborn door.

THE IMMORTAL

The slight stoop, the bifocals he refused to wear in company, and the slack hammocks of wrinkles across his face all indicated that Martin Drennan was indeed old—already past the hundred and ten mark, if, as he insisted, he could remember the Franco-Prussian war of 1870. The officials sent out to him by the Department of Social Welfare would usually nod agreeably up to this point, allowing for Drennan's obviously advanced but undetermined years, and his healthy imagination. However, even in good mood, and having managed to make the pleasant ten-minute journey to the old man's house take most of the normally office-bound morning, they could by no means tolerate his claim that he could recall the sunny afternoon of the Battle of Waterloo.

'Most people stopped believing in immortality back in the Middle Ages, Mr Drennan.' Black felt like adding, 'Perhaps you remember?' but decided he was wasting his time.

'It was the day after my father's birthday, that's how I remember it—June the 18th, eighteen hundred and fifteen—a scorcher as they'd say in these parts....'

Black stuffed his papers in a folder and left the musty cottage, and after his car had splattered itself with cow dung, and finally reached the single tarmacadam road which connected this web of dust and dung tracks with the neighbouring small-town world, only the tired and somewhat sad voice of Martin Drennan could be heard recalling aloud his memories of a day one hundred and fifty-eight years before.

The following morning brought winter, and the sky seemed almost to vibrate in trying to contain the clouds which tumbled together with the threat of storm. Drennan had never been a religious man, hobbling off to church only when he felt it was better to placate the parish priest rather than have him calling round feigning a desire for chat. Yet he had no small faith in the sky as oracle and guide, and as he cycled into town he watched it spread its clouds for his attention.

It was his first visit to the small midland town in a long time. The streets seemed narrower, cluttered with advertisements. Banks and building societies had replaced the intimate groceries, flower shops and butchers. He leaned his bicycle against a lamp-post and entered a pub where men with pints and dripping candles were singing the joys of electricity blackouts—a sign of the storm that was on its way—their shadows huge and threatening as clouds across the ceiling. Drennan smiled to himself that in his primitive cottage without modern conveniences he had not known the outside world too had been left in darkness.

'A stout, please,' he called, timidly.

When age had handed him his retirement papers all those years before, he had abandoned the smoke and

101

peculiar comfort of being a mercenary and devoted himself instead to the camera and a world of frozen people, quaint motorcars and eerie portraits of old bonnetted ladies, their hands chalk-white and twisted in their laps like roots. And now he whittled animals from mahogany or, when money was scarce, from red deal, and they fetched modest sums at Sales of Work, parish auctions, and a stall at the Abbeyleix Maytime Festival— little dogs, cats and elegant birds with spindly legs and mantelpiece expressions. The energy which once had fuelled his soldiering and travelling now became the energy of creativity—but also of a vague apprehension that seemed to coincide with the approach of winter.

The barman centred the drink on a round beer-mat and stacked the change in a tapering column beside a Santa Claus candle, hints of what had been a pink face still visible in the pool of clothing at its feet.

'It's Christmas here all year round,' laughed a toothless old lad in the corner, sensing Drennan's bewilderment.

Drennan sipped his stout, left the froth on his lips to dry with a tickling sensation—it seemed a lifetime since he'd felt that cool kiss.

'Drennan, isn't it?' A bearded face emerged from the shadow.

Drennan nodded.

'Tony Black—my son's with the Department. I hear you're not a young man.'

Drennan gave him a puzzled look.

'What I mean is, not as young as you look.' He was staring at Drennan's eyes as if he were counting the rings around them in an attempt to calculate the new arrival's age.

'I hear,' he said, 'I hear,' and then he almost shouted, 'I hear you're a hundred and eighty!'

Drennan gritted his teeth. He knew the dangers of replying, but he also knew he couldn't stop himself trying to explain his situation, as much to capture the mystery of it in words for himself as to communicate to this Black fellow and his candlelight associates.

'It started in the seventies...' he began.

'Would that be the eighteen seventies or the nineteen seventies?' said a voice.

Drennan looked up and saw men with candles, and men with candles reflected in whiskey mirrors.

'The eighteen seventies.' He forced it out; and in the darkness bar-stools were drawn nearer over the tiled floor, and cigarettes looped like fireflies.

He told the story of how he had lived in Paris, how he'd stayed in a dark, cobble-stoned region, spending most of his nights in candlelit bars like this one, smoking cigars and discussing literature with a group of serious young students who would arrive stately on big black bicycles and leave wavering side to side, but never falling, in the narrow streets that were barely wider than the span of a man's arms. How they would talk then, sometimes until dawn, about *Les Fleurs du Mal,* argue about the decadence of Zola's *Thérèse Raquin,* or discuss painting, particularly Cezanne who was a favourite among such groups who considered themselves outside the mainstream of the artistic world.

Drennan looked up for a moment at the confused faces around him. Then he continued.

It had been in one of those bars that he had had his attack. He remembered little of the actual event. The room had spun and he had come to some three months later with a young nurse by his bedside. He recalled climbing slowly out of bed, his limbs almost powerless, and hobbling over to a mirror. His face was unevenly shaven, with small cuts along the hard edge of his chin; his skin was white and looked as if it might fall away if tugged. But somehow he looked stronger, and even younger, despite it all. He'd staggered back to bed, not finally leaving the house or his silent nurse until he'd spent a week making unsteady tours of the rooms, and attempting morning and evening squats in the manner of a retired colonel. He'd moved to a small attic where his time was spent trying to figure out what was happening to him: he seemed to have stopped ageing! His eyes were still bright, and his hair was as black as it had been when he was a boy. But that made little sense: he was seventy-three, maybe seventy-four. He'd spent the greater part of his life fighting in indecisive wars, and had come to Paris to pass what he'd expected to be his final years. And now, to his astonishment, he realized that that had been almost a century before!

There was a terrible silence in the pub. The electricity had come back on unremarked. Pints had gone flat on all the tables.

'Do you mean to say you're not getting older like the rest of us common townsfolk?' asked Black.

'Not in the last hundred years,' replied Drennan, taking a sip from his glass, a movement that seemed to rouse the pub from its rapture. Anxiously he scratched the side of his bristled face as his audience bustled off to the toilets, mumbling.

Only Black and Drennan remained at the table.

'And how might you explain that?' asked the former. 'I mean if I was to push you for an explanation.'

'Well,' said Drennan, 'there's God and angels... and maybe a mistake was made. That's how I like to see it....'

'Are you saying in Heaven?' Black was beginning to lose patience with the rambling eccentric.

'And sometimes I suspect that there may have been something I never did, a food I never ate.... Maybe I've avoided ageing by some... coincidence.'

Black blew, an exaggerated sigh, like a trumpeter warming up. But he settled down when Drennan paid him no attention. Drennan continued.

'Then, when I began to suspect that I'd been overlooked, I made up my mind to continue travelling, to change occupation as often as possible.'

He took an important mouthful of porter.

'If you want me to say it, I've been trying to cloud over the facts with illogical decisions, in an attempt to guarantee my pass to eternity.' He had tried his best to lighten the mood.

'Is... that... so?'

'But now I've had enough. I want to settle down like everyone else, potter around, fit in somewhere.'

Black leered and held out his hand for a handshake:

'You'll fit in just fine here, Martin.'

Drennan gave him a thankful, but weak smile.

Black stood. 'Sure aren't most of us on this side of the street well over the two-hundred mark ourselves? You're only a youngster!'

The pub burst into applause. Black disappeared off towards the toilets like a comedian who knows he should exit following his best line. By the time he came back, crouched and zipping, Drennan had gone.

Snow had fallen in a graveyard. Old headstones were stuck into it at odd angles like arrows in a corpse. The only thing clearly defined was the black wound of a newly-dug hole.

In the morning, Drennan awoke to a farm frozen—puddles solidified, mud crusted, a greyness in place of the sky, and the ground littered with frost as if a child had tugged his kite string and brought the sky crashing down in shards of glass.

Small things preyed on his mind—place-names, vivid memories of former inhabitants. And while pondering the origins of the Dead Wall, the Robber's Well, Timahoe, he began to lose faith in his memory, began to doubt that it was really his own. Was Black right? Had he ever been to Africa, ever seen the Battle of Waterloo? Or had the 'memories' just been passed on to him by tipsy old boys and well worn, second-hand books? Were crazed pigs streaking and squealing down the Main Street the recollections of the old grocer in the corner shop, or his own? Could what had seemed to be his own really have been the collective memories of the people of the townland where he grew up and was influenced? And, if this was true, how could it ever be possible to see again himself or it in perspective? How strange it was to be back and find himself ordained an eccentric by these people whose history occupied his every waking hour. They'd just laughed when he'd confronted them with a living piece of their heritage.

Drennan lay in bed, watching the first snows fall, conjuring the faces of animals he knew he would never carve.

THE GRASS ROOTS

Seamus and Deirdre left the children with her parents—
along with reminders about bedtime, favourite foods,
and guide-lines as to the number of hours of homework
in relation to hours of television (according to someone
on one of those health programmes). Deirdre kissed
everyone in the room, including her mother whom she
had hardly touched in the eight years since she had
married Seamus—'a pipe cleaner who doesn't smoke', in
her mother's opinion. Seamus watched the whole
proceedings with amusement, smiling sickly at Mrs
Winch and telling Deirdre afterwards in the car:

'Holy God, woman, you'd think we were going away
for ever.'

For Deirdre, this was exactly how it felt. This was the
first time she had left the kids for anything longer than a
few hours. And although a weekend 150 miles away in a
Galway hotel was hardly an eternity, the undiscussed
horror in her mother's eyes as she took control of her
charges had sown the seeds of sleepless night in Deirdre,
seeds that were probably already sprouting before she
was out of sight of the country house. Even as they drove
out of the small midland town, she was considering gifts

for the exhausted parents she expected to find on her return—not to mention the irritable children.

Not that some part of her did not secretly welcome this break from urban married life—in fact, the prospect of a weekend to themselves filled her with an enthusiasm she had not known since her college days, and one *he* had never known. However, the nature and purpose of the trip equally filled her with apprehensions, and she noted to herself that Seamus was already beginning to speak about the children in the past tense, and in that perfectly balanced and unnatural politician's tone. She began to worry about her appearance in an attempt to change the subject of her fears, and found herself dreading the protracted introductions that always took the first hour or two of these gatherings. She could hear his colleagues commenting, discretely, on 'the little woman's intelligence', her dress sense—before, that is, they shoo'd her off into some other room full of political wives while the menfolk got on with the serious business of decision making or exchanged catch-phrases over gin and tonics in the yellowy light of the bar.

'Yes, Tom, but there is no party without the grass roots.'

'True, Shay, but what you gain on the swings you lose on the roundabouts.'

The rain started as the car passed into the countryside.

In Stradbally, unconcerned about the weather, the kids began by searching for frogs to inflate. Aidan, who was the elder, went equipped with drinking straws (which he called strinking straws) and bicycle pump, and Siobhán followed, bringing her copy-book to practise 'joinedy writing' should the afternoon's events bore or upset, or simply disgust, her as usual. Nevertheless, she would not, in such unfamiliar surroundings, let her brother out of her sights.

Granny had packed a lunch of ham and cheese sandwiches and a shiny red apple each, the kind that kids hate and grannies love. Fifty pence weighed with possibility in Aidan's pocket, and Siobhán carried like a cudgel the tulip grandad had timidly given her, frightened by the threat of puberty which had appeared in her eyes since he had last seen her some years before.

After the sweet shop they had headed towards the river fields, smiling beatifically at the school teacher who waved from her car—all but swooning over the sight of strange children—Aidan blowing bubbles and all the while imagining frogs filled with helium drifting above the clouds, their eyes full of wondrous horror. He imagined a mattress made of inflated frogs, floating him up to where he could see the shopping trolleys dumped in the river rushes and the teenage boys with catapults, practising on crows behind the cemetery walls.

Siobhán was thinking of the letter *f,* wondering if it should twist left or right under the blue line, or why either way should make any difference if she knew which was which and why couldn't *g's* go round and round inside like a snail's shell so long as *she* knew what it meant?

They climbed a fence and vanished into a limitless countryside.

Deirdre and Seamus had arrived at their hotel and Seamus was already in high spirits at the bar discussing election strategies, percentages, whips (!), swinging votes, angling licences and, of course, gin and tonics. Deirdre was drinking Ballygowan Sparkling Spring Water and trying to keep her eyes away from the telephone. She also found herself remembering the last time they had been to a hotel together, in Killarney, their fifth wedding anniversary weekend, when she had appeared from the bathroom in her white laced négligé to find him sat up reading a report on badger extermination in the north midlands. This time around— whether he had seen to it or not—there were two single beds in the room, and although he had said he would have something done about it, nothing had in fact been done and she did not want to cause gossip among the hotel staff by repeating the request to the receptionist. She wondered when the time came if she would have the courage to pull the two beds together, as they had done secretly in their student days in his mother's house. But on further consideration she was not sure if separate sleeping arrangements were not part of these political 'away weekends' where 'the little woman' was a compulsory accessory to be worn like a Fáinne or a pioneer pin.

The Virginity of Politics. She swore she would write that book. Perhaps, she thought, she had really agreed to come on this weekend to research that very work, to make an in-depth investigation into the carry-on of elected representatives and would-bes behind closed hotel doors.

She looked over at Seamus, his legs splayed before him on the bar stool. How little of the country boy Dublin had erased from his make-up, even after thirteen years! How predictable he had become—or always was; how middle-aged already. She looked over at Mulligan, the fat, bearded aggressive wing of the party, and then to his 'missus' who was reading *Cosmopolitan* by the tropical fish tank.

What do you think, Mrs. Mulligan? Deirdre imagined herself asking. Virgins or prostitutes?

Perhaps sensing Deirdre's attentions, Mrs. Mulligan looked up from her magazine and smiled sweetly, in her eyes the sadness of a middle-aged woman confronted by beautiful youth.

The grass was up to Siobhán's knees and there were a few too many insects for her liking. Suddenly something was on her neck.

'Aidan!'

Her brother came back nonchalantly to his sister's side, as weary as a soldier, or his father playing football.

'Yeah. What?'

Siobhán pointed to her shoulder.

His eyes lit up. 'Don't move.'

'Aidan!'

Kneeling in the grass, he produced his knife, grinned at her and put it back away in his pocket. Then he took a small pill container from his jacket pocket, removed the lid and moved slowly towards her.

In a moment it was all over: the ladybird was in the container, the lid was on and the only trace of the operation was the smirk on Aidan's face. Deirdre bent to remove a briar from her ankle sock and saw that she had torn the skin.

'Look at my blood, Aidan,' she said.

'Yeah,' he said, full of admiration for the first wound of the day.

By six o'clock that evening Granny Reilly was beginning to feel concerned. Every few minutes she went to the window. Grandad, smoking his pipe and watching a round-up of the week's news, exclaimed once in a while at the ferocity of the nation, its unparalleled crimes and degradations. He would forget that he was watching a compilation of past horrors and regularly was heard to gasp: 'Not again, not another six soldiers,' or 'That Duchess of York! How does she do it?' Granny Reilly looked at the happy mother on the screen and then at her husband crouched in his armchair. Behind her his supper of bacon, sausage and egg solidified under the grill where it would sit until he had had enough of the world.

'Martin, do you think...'

'I don't,' he said, without looking up.

'If they knew the countryside...' continued Granny Reilly, looking out through her own reflection into the encroaching evening.

Grandad Reilly turned from the latest joyrider report and looked at his wife with incomprehension.

'If they can survive in *that* open asylum'—he blew one nostril into his handkerchief—'they'll survive Stradbally.'

Granny, despite the evidence, was not convinced.

If the evening went well for Deirdre in the hotel, it was because she had broken all of the unspoken rules for delegates' wives—and a few of the spoken ones as well. It was now just after ten and she was already pleasantly sozzled in the lounge where two traditional musicians were playing against the conversation, and at least one of them was wondering if this enthusiastic young woman in the red dress was free-floating, even on a temporary basis. Fortunately it was the older, somewhat less attractive one who was expressing, or at least appeared to be expressing, an interest in her. And so Deirdre felt no qualms about returning the flirtatious smile, even the odd wink, knowing it would come to nothing, except perhaps another rum and black during the interval.

Seamus, of course, was by now nowhere to be seen. Up in the war room kissing plaster dolls, Deirdre supposed, and laughed aloud. Most of the other wives, or whatever they were, had gone to bed. And Mrs. Mulligan's *Cosmo* lay face down beside the fish tank as if the piranhas had finally been unable to resist her generous proportions.

Oh, life was a fine thing all right, full of surprise. The kids were by now safely gorged on greasy rubbish and ice-cream and were dreaming of Kylie Minogue and Jason Donovan and Teenage Mutant Hero/Ninja Turtles. When they went to sleep they went to a heaven reserved for pre-pubescents, a hell for anyone over the age of ten.

Deirdre was delighted with this unexpected feeling of relief, of frivolity, which crept though her intoxicated limbs. Winking again at the musician who was lapping away at a pint of Guinness through his beard, she vowed to get away in future just as often as she could. She was now seriously considering her idea of a book on the whole childish affairxxxx. Well, perhaps not seriously.

It was almost nine, a half hour since Grandad Reilly had reluctantly agreed to go look for the kids. He had taken a flashlight and his walking stick, together with a bag of cough drops and his pipe, and had left promising, yes, if he found no sign he would call to the sergeant's house but , no, he didn't want to go creating a big fuss about nothing.

Granny Reilly sat in the kitchen listening to the clock. Though she was beside the telephone she did not dare look at it.

By now the sergeant and his eldest son—a technology student in Limerick, home for the weekend to see his girlfriend—had been press-ganged into joining in the search.

What was the little girl wearing? Grandad Reilly could not remember. If he had been asked to describe his own clothes there in the dark he would not have known if he had his brown shoes or his black bootees on. And the little boy? Here too his memory drew a blank after the word 'jeans'.

After a number of such questions, all the sergeant had managed to ascertain was that they were young city kids who had never been lost in the countryside before, and that they possibly had red hair.

'Possibly?' The sergeant leaned close, expecting alcohol on Grandad Reilly's breath.

'Well,' shrugged the other, producing spectacles from his top left pocket as if this were sufficient explanation.

The search party of three moved off after a moment, calling 'Aidan!' and 'Siobhán!' and 'Over here!', with Grandad Reilly muttering, 'Where? Can't see a blasted thing.'

Deirdre and Seamus lay on their separate beds looking at their separate pieces of ceiling overhead. How had it come to this? Deirdre wondered—though she knew the answer. What leap of imagination would it have taken for him to have moved one or other of the beds while she was still in the bathroom? How could he lie there now pretending to be asleep when she could perfectly well see the whites of his eyes in the light from outside the window?

Deirdre was already nearing the end of the first chapter of her fictionalized exposé, already answering the questions of shocked tv journalists—'Is it really...' 'Can you stand by...'—always with the same cool answer: 'Read the book, gentlemen. It's all there'—when suddenly the telephone rang. Immediately she flew into a panic when she found she could not move.

Seamus shot upright on his hearing his name called, and switched on the light between their beds.

'Hello?' he said, snatching up the receiver. 'Yes, what is it?'

Deirdre waited.

'And goodnight to you too.' He hung up.

'Well?' she asked when he offered no report. 'Who was it?'

'Your mother,' said Seamus, irritably, scratching his head. 'She says the kids are asleep.'

Just before midnight, as Granny Reilly had begun her fourth rosary, the door had opened and in had walked Siobhán and Aidan, along with Grandad and the sergeant and the sergeant's son.

'Lost,' said Grandad, heading for his forgotten tobacco pouch.

'There were no lights or anything,' said Aidan, defensively. 'No wonder animals sleep all the time.'

'I have a red ring,' said Siobhán, standing before Granny. Granny suggested a decade of the Rosary.

The sergeant bid everyone goodnight. His son followed him, dragging his feet and looking as if he would probably drag them all the next day about the house while his parents rushed for Sunday mass and he packed for the afternoon train back to Limerick.

In the circumstances, Granny had decided it was better not to mention the telephone call.

Seamus awoke in the morning to find Deirdre naked beside him. It came as quite a surprise, as did the négligé which he seemed to recognize. He lay there looking at her red hair on the pillow, his hand on her belly.

In her dream, Deirdre presented a female president with a signed copy of her book.